If she were to settle down, it would take a special kind of guy, one who was as adventurous as she was

Sara had to admit Reece didn't strike her as the least bit adventurous. He was ultraserious, a buttoned-down CPA who loved to talk about risk management and long-term projections.

Her projections usually didn't extend past what she planned to have for lunch that day.

And yet…he was so delicious. Not only that, but he was a good guy. Delicious men came and went, but ones with character—they were a bit more rare.

Maybe she ought to decide what she wanted from Reece before she did something crazy.

Dear Reader,

Alpha heroes—those arrogant, I'm-in-control-here males—certainly have their appeal. Or those dark, brooding, wounded heroes…I love 'em! But give me a man with brains over brawn and I completely melt.

Reece Remington is just such a man. Unlike his take-charge cousin Cooper (from *Reluctant Partners*, the first in the SECOND SONS series) or his devil-may-care ladies' man cousin Max (whom you'll meet in the third book of the trilogy, *The Good Father*), Reece is a man more comfortable with a computer spreadsheet than a woman. He's handsome as sin, but hides behind his glasses. He always plays it safe. He needs a woman to wake him up and teach him to enjoy life, but he doesn't know that, either! What fun I had matching up Reece with happy-go-lucky Sara.

My editor said, "I love all the Remington men, but I have a soft spot for Reece." That's how I feel, too. If I were going to marry any of the Remingtons in real life, Reece would be my choice. I hope you love him as much as I do. (And maybe I'm like Sara more than I'd care to admit!)

All best,

Kara Lennox

The Pregnancy Surprise
KARA LENNOX

HARLEQUIN®

TORONTO • NEW YORK • LONDON
AMSTERDAM • PARIS • SYDNEY • HAMBURG
STOCKHOLM • ATHENS • TOKYO • MILAN • MADRID
PRAGUE • WARSAW • BUDAPEST • AUCKLAND

ISBN-13: 978-0-373-75244-7
ISBN-10:   0-373-75244-X

THE PREGNANCY SURPRISE

www.eHarlequin.com

Printed in U.S.A.

ABOUT THE AUTHOR

Texas native Kara Lennox has earned her living at various times as an art director, typesetter, textbook editor and reporter. She's worked in a boutique, a health club and an ad agency. She's been an antiques dealer and even a blackjack dealer. But no work has made her happier than writing romance novels. She has written more than fifty books.

When not writing, Kara indulges in an ever-changing array of hobbies. Her latest passions are bird-watching and long-distance bicycling. She loves to hear from readers; you can visit her Web page at www.karalennox.com.

Books by Kara Lennox

HARLEQUIN AMERICAN ROMANCE

Chapter One

The crash from the kitchen was so loud, it sounded like a car coming through the wall.

Sara Kaufman's heart hammered inside her chest as she dropped her dust cloth and ran toward the noise.

"Help! Sara, are you there?"

It was Miss Greer. The thready voice calling for help confirmed Sara's worst fears. Her elderly employer was hurt.

Sara reached the kitchen door at the same time as Reece Remington, one of the guests at the Sunsetter Bed-and-Breakfast where Sara lived and worked. They bumped each other trying to fit through the door side by side.

Reece stepped back and let Sara enter first. "Was that Miss Greer?" Concern etched his handsome face.

Sara was about to answer, but Miss Greer called again. "Sara?" The voice came from the open pantry. "Is that you?"

"I'm coming, Miss Greer!" Sara and Reece rushed to the pantry. Through the doorway they could see their white-haired landlady lying amidst an avalanche of boxes and canned goods. Flour covered her face—it looked as if an open bag of the stuff had fallen on her head.

"Oh, my God, what happened?" Sara's first instinct was to reach for Miss Greer and get her back on her feet, but Reece stopped her with a hand to her shoulder.

"Don't move her," he said. "If she's injured, that might make things worse."

"What happened?" Sara asked again.

"I'm not sure." The elderly lady sounded less panicked now that help had arrived. "Maybe I slipped on something. When I started to fall, I grabbed the shelf and pulled half the pantry down on top of me and now I'm stuck. Thank goodness it was the flour that hit me in the head, rather than the economy-size can of cling peaches."

"Are you injured, Miss Greer?" Reece asked. "Does anything hurt?"

"Now, don't fuss over me," she groused, moving her head around so they could see she at least hadn't broken her neck. "I think I can stand up if you two help."

Sara and Reece both squeezed into the pantry. It was a tight fit, with all three of them in there, and under other circumstances Sara would have enjoyed the proximity. Reece was a thoroughly delicious man, tall and rangy with broad shoulders showcased perfectly by the starched, button-down shirts he wore. If only he would relax a little…

Reece took one of Miss Greer's arms and Sara took the other, and they tried to pull her up. But they'd moved her only a few inches when she howled in pain and they were forced to gently set her back down.

"Where does it hurt?" Sara asked.

"My hip."

"I'm calling an ambulance." Reece exited the pantry, which at least made it easier for Sara to breathe in there. All that maleness crammed into such a small space was a little distracting.

"I'm sure it's not serious," Sara said, though she wasn't sure at all.

It scared Sara to see Miss Greer like this.

Sara had worked at the Port Clara, Texas, B and B for more than ten years. The older woman wasn't just her boss; she was family.

"What am I going to do?" Miss Greer asked. "What if I've broken something? You hear about old people breaking their hips and never coming home again."

Sara wished she had an answer, or even some believably reassuring words, but she'd never been much good in an emergency. All she could think to do was hold Miss Greer's hand and squeeze it.

Reece was already on the phone. He was calm, no sign of panic, and Sara took several deep breaths, trying to follow suit. The paramedics would come, and maybe they would determine it wasn't a serious injury.

Then they could all laugh over the mishap, and Sara could clean up the pantry, fix the broken shelf and make soup and sandwiches for everyone.

She was glad Reece was here. He obviously knew how to handle a crisis.

She squeezed Miss Greer's hand again. "How bad does it hurt?"

"It's not too bad if I lie still," the old lady said, but her brow was creased with tension.

Sara nibbled at her lower lip. Maybe Miss Greer's hip wasn't broken. Maybe she'd just...sprained it or something.

Reece returned and got down on his knees beside Sara. "The ambulance is on its way, Miss Greer. Can we do anything to make you more comfortable while we wait?"

"I suppose I should get ready for a hospital stay," Miss Greer grumbled. "Sara, you go pack me a bag. I want my own nightgown so I don't have to wear one of those things that's open down the back so everyone can ogle your hindquarters. Reece, you go find my pocketbook. I'll need my Medicare card."

The woman gave orders like a general.

"One of us should stay with you," Sara said.

"Why? I'm not going anywhere."

Sara exchanged a look with Reece as she pushed to her feet, and tried not to smile. Miss Greer must not be in too bad a shape if she could still be ornery.

Sara had only been in Miss Greer's bedroom a couple of times in all the years she had worked there. Her landlady was intensely private. The room was as neat and clean as a monk's cell. Sara hunted around until she found an overnight case on the top shelf of the closet.

She reached for it, but it was a few inches too high.

"Let me get that." Reece came up behind her and stretched his arms over her head, easily reaching the case. She felt the heat of his body almost, but not quite, touching her back, and her skin tingled with awareness.

Whether he meant to or not, he'd tempted her since he and his two cousins had moved into the B and B a few weeks ago to deal with an inheritance from their uncle.

Reece handed her the small, cloth-covered case. "Here you go. Do you know where her purse is?"

Sara looked around. "Ah. Hanging on the hook on the back of the door."

She opened the dresser and haphazardly filled the suitcase with nightgowns, underwear and socks, because Miss Greer's feet were always cold, even in summer. Reece, the fake alligator purse clutched between his large hands, watched her.

"What?" she said. "You think I'm doing it wrong?"

"She might like her clothes folded."

"You think I should fold Miss Greer's underwear?"

"She obviously likes things neat. Maybe you should pack a robe, too. And a toothbrush."

"You want to do this?" she asked Reece, who seemed not entirely comfortable amid all the accoutrements of an old lady. He looked excruciatingly out of place surrounded by cabbage roses, lace doilies and the faint scent of violet water.

"No, no. I guess you're doing fine."

Apparently not, given his suggestions. "Why don't you check on Miss Greer? I'll be done in a minute."

She did not need help packing—she did it all the time. Her best friend, Allie, teased Sara that she could live for six months in the Amazon with only what she could stuff into her backpack.

When Sara finished cramming the overnight case with everything she thought might come in handy, she returned to the kitchen, but she paused in the doorway to watch Reece and Miss Greer. He brushed flour off the elderly woman's face using a handkerchief and a gentle touch. Sara couldn't hear what he said to her, but his voice was low and soothing.

Miss Greer watched him with obvious adoration on her face. She reached up to pat his cheek, and he squeezed her bony hand, sandwiching it between his and holding it there, looking comfortable with the display of affection.

The slight irritation she'd felt toward Reece vanished. Any man who could show kindness and affection to an old lady who wasn't even a blood relative—and look at ease doing so—was okay in her book.

Miss Greer treated him like a favorite grandson, and Reece sometimes even made the gruff old woman smile.

Sara strode into the kitchen. "Here's your overnight bag. Can I do anything else? Do you want something to eat?" Nothing was hopeless if you had a big bowl of spicy tortilla soup in front of you, along with a thick slice of homemade bread and real butter.

"Thank you, dear," Miss Greer said, "but I can't eat right now. What am I going to do? A broken hip is serious business. I'll be out of commission for weeks, and who's going to run the B and B, I ask you, if I'm in the hospital? I have guests arriving today—six people!"

"Don't worry about that," Sara said. "I can handle things until you're back on your feet."

"What about your trip to California?" Miss Greer asked. "Anyway, the B and B is a full-time job and I can't afford to pay you a salary. You do more than your fair share, given that I'm only paying you room and board."

Sara did need money to live on, which meant she had to work other jobs sometimes, like the temporary gig providing meals at an independent movie shoot in California.

"That job has been postponed," she said breezily.

"But what about the business end?" Miss Greer asked, a note of desperation creeping into her voice. "Sure, you can clean, and the customers seem to like the breakfasts you've cooked, but you're a disaster with finances."

Sara tried not to take offense at the blunt comment. She knew this wasn't an indictment of her trustworthiness, but confirmation of the fact that she was dreadful when it came to managing money. Everybody knew that. If there was such a thing as numbers dyslexia, she had it.

"Please try not to worry," Sara said. "We'll work something out. Hey, I know. Reece could handle the money side."

"Excuse me?" Reece said, giving her a panicked look.

"He's here anyway," Sara continued as if he hadn't objected, "and he's a CPA, so you can be sure he's competent. He's doing all the bookkeeping for Remington Charters, and you know Allie wouldn't allow that if he wasn't good with money."

"Oh, would you, Reece?" Miss Greer asked. "You're such a good guest, and I hate to impose when you and your cousins have been so nice, but I would rest easy knowing…knowing Sara doesn't have to handle everything."

Reece removed his glasses and rubbed one eye before answering. "Well…sure, I can do that for you.

But I'll be going back to New York next week. If I don't return soon, I'll lose my job."

Next week?

"I thought your family owned the company," Sara said. "Isn't your boss your father? He wouldn't fire you."

"You obviously don't know my father."

"Don't you still have lots of vacation left?" she asked him. Cooper, Reece's cousin, had said this was Reece's first vacation in eight years. Eight years! How did he stand it, the same job, crunching numbers day after day after day?

"I hadn't planned to use it all," he said. "But don't worry, Miss Greer. I'll stay for at least a few more days, and if you need to be in the hospital longer than that, we'll work something out."

The doorbell rang.

"That must be the paramedics," Sara said as she went to answer it.

Reece tried not to feel annoyed that Sara had volunteered him for a job before consulting him, knowing he couldn't refuse in front of a woman lying on the floor with a broken hip.

"Just promise me you won't leave the finances to Sara," Miss Greer whispered. "Don't get me wrong, she's a lovely girl, sweet and generous to a fault and a hard worker. But she doesn't have a head for business. Have you ever seen her checkbook? It's the stuff of my nightmares."

Reece couldn't help it, he actually shuddered. He'd caught a glimpse of Sara's checkbook when she'd brought it out to pay one of her hippie-artist friends for a handmade ceramic teapot—an entirely useless item in his opinion, but Sara had been in raptures about it. The checkbook register was written in five different colors of ink and had more cross-outs than a third-grader's book report.

"I know exactly what you mean," Reece whispered back.

"You can't let her touch the B and B's checkbook—or the calendar. She'll write down the wrong dates."

"I'll handle it, promise," Reece said. "You focus on getting well."

Miss Greer pinched his cheek. He hadn't let anyone get away with pinching his cheek since he was eight years old. "You're a good boy, and so handsome, too. How is it no woman has caught you?"

A few had tried, especially after a radio station had named him one of the top-twenty bachelors in Manhattan. But he suspected most of them had been more entranced with the cachet of the Remington family name than with Reece himself.

The truth was, he liked living alone. He liked having everything just so, and the one time he'd gotten close enough to a woman that she'd halfway moved in with him, it had driven him crazy.

"She's in here." Sara directed the paramedics into the kitchen, where they had Miss Greer on a stretcher in no time. The older woman didn't complain, but Reece could tell by the tension in her face that she was in pain.

"We'll follow in Reece's car," Sara said, patting Miss Greer's arm as the stretcher passed by her.

Reece waited until the stretcher had cleared the kitchen door. "We will?" he said to Sara.

"Of course we will."

"Shouldn't we call someone from Miss Greer's family?"

"She doesn't have any family. She's never married or had children. And we can't let her go to the hospital by herself."

"I thought I would stay here and clean up the mess in the pantry," Reece said, "and fix the shelf. Shouldn't one of us be here to take care of the guests?"

"The guests know where we hide the key. They've all stayed with us before, so it's no big deal. But if you want to stay here I guess that's okay."

"Isn't it kind of unsettling, just letting strangers into your house to roam about?"

Sara laughed. He loved to hear her laugh, the sound a bell-like tinkling. "You New Yorkers! You think the Silversteins are going to steal us blind when we have their credit-card information?"

Good point. He nodded.

"Anyway, B and B guests are nice people in general. That's what I've found. They never steal anything."

Personally, Reece thought Sara was far too trusting—of everyone. The way she wandered all over the world, crashing wherever someone offered her a bed, sharing meals at the homes of people she barely knew, anyone could take advantage of her.

But she would never believe him. Something bad would have to happen before she would become suspicious and skeptical like him.

He frowned at the thought. He liked her innocence. It was part of what made Sara, Sara.

"So can I borrow your car?" she asked.

"You don't have a car?" Come to think of it, he'd never seen her drive. He'd seen her ride off on a battered bicycle, but he hadn't imagined that was her only transportation.

"Mine broke down when I was driving back from Santa Fe, and I couldn't afford the repair bill, so I sold it and rode the bus the rest of the way home."

"How do you survive without one?"

"Port Clara's not that big. I walk or ride my bike, and now that the streetcar is running again, I ride that. But the hospital is all the way in Corpus Christi. So can I borrow your car?"

The thought pained him. He'd just bought that car— a cream puff of a Mercedes, barely used. He'd been thinking about buying a car anyway, and he'd intended to purchase something conservative and practical. But the little blue Mercedes had caught his eye.

He seldom succumbed to impulse purchases, and the car was unlike anything he'd ever owned, but he hadn't been able to walk away from it.

He hadn't even let his cousin Max drive it.

"All right, I'll go to the hospital with you," he said to Sara. Miss Greer would probably appreciate someone there to handle the paperwork, he reasoned.

When they were settled into the Mercedes's leather bucket seats, Reece entered their destination in his satellite navigation system and they were off. The GPS routed them over the causeway that linked their little barrier island with the mainland, which was a relief. He always felt nauseous on the ferry, which was the other way off the island.

"I've been dying to ride in this car," Sara confessed. "Do you like it?"

"So far." It was the most sinfully decadent car he'd ever bought.

"Why didn't you hire someone to drive your car down from New York, like Cooper did?"

"I didn't own a car. With the cost of parking and maintenance in Manhattan, using public transportation or taxis makes more fiscal sense. I'll probably end up selling this one."

"But what if you want to take a Sunday drive? Or a road trip?"

"It's easy to lease a car if you really need one." But he hadn't taken a road trip since college, and even back then he hadn't seen the point in it.

"I miss my car," she said wistfully. "It had over two hundred thousand miles, and I logged every one of them."

"Maybe time to get a new one then. Old cars aren't as safe as the new ones, and not as economical or environmentally friendly, either."

"Yeah, well, if I could buy a new one I would. I'll have to settle for a used one, once I save enough money."

At least she understood the concept of saving money. A lot of people didn't—they wanted to buy everything on credit.

He wondered how people like Sara made it in the world. She was obviously not stupid. She was pretty—

more than pretty, actually—and personable. He knew not everyone had been born with the advantages he had, and maybe her parents hadn't sent her to college, but there were lots of careers that didn't require a degree.

She could have gone into sales, or gotten an entry-level job at a company and worked her way up. But instead she'd chosen to drift aimlessly—at least, that was the way it appeared to him. He doubted she had any savings or property. "Have you made any plans for retirement?" he asked suddenly.

She stared at him as if he'd just sprouted an extra nose. "Excuse me? I'm twenty-nine. I haven't planned for next month."

"Now is the perfect time to start thinking about it. If you saved just a hundred dollars a month—"

"What is this? You're not going to try to sell me swampland in Florida, are you?"

Obviously he'd made a conversational gaffe. "I just worry about you."

"Oh." She backed down a bit. "Well, that's sweet, but *I* don't worry about me, so why should you?"

"Exactly."

His answer seemed to flummox her. "You hardly know me."

"We've lived under the same roof for almost three weeks now. I know you better than you think."

She smiled and cocked her head flirtatiously. "And here I thought you didn't know I was alive. You hardly ever say anything to me."

That was because she often made him tongue-tied. It certainly wasn't because he didn't notice her. With her swirly, bright-colored skirts and tie-dyed shirts and big, dangly earrings, how could anyone miss her? Not to mention that mountain of curly brown hair and those big, soft hazel eyes.

She was watching him carefully with those incredible eyes, and his mind went blank. Talking about finances, he was in safe territory. Anything else, and it was hit or miss.

"I didn't mean to shut you down," she said. "If you really want to tell me about how I should save for retirement, I'll listen."

He shook his head. "Never mind. I overstepped. I apologize."

Neither of them said a word the rest of the way to Corpus Christi.

Chapter Two

Sara knew she'd blown it. She'd finally engaged Reece in a conversation—a real conversation, not just *Would you like more coffee?* or *Thanks for breakfast.*

But she'd gotten her back up because he'd asked her about her future, and she had a reflexive defense mechanism built in about that. Every time she visited her parents, they hammered her about how she chose to live her life.

Reece obviously disapproved of her, too. When he'd said he worried about her she'd softened, but it was too late—her reaction had sent him right back into strong-and-silent mode.

She wondered what to do next. She'd never been timid where men were concerned, and if she saw one she liked, she let him know, and she persisted until she found out whether there was any interest in her.

The jury was still out with Reece. She hadn't flirted openly with him, since Miss Greer would not have approved of her hitting on guests. Yet she felt a certain chemistry at work whenever they were in the same room.

Once they reached the hospital, Sara sat in Miss Greer's treatment room while Reece took care of the paperwork. He stuck his head in the door once to see how their patient was doing, but then he disappeared again.

Maybe he didn't like being around sick people. But when he returned a short time later with a doctor in tow, insisting that he take a look at Miss Greer *now,* she realized he was just doing his man thing—solving problems, making things happen. She had tried to snag a doctor in the hallway—twice—but they'd blown her off. She was doubly glad she'd insisted on Reece coming to the hospital, or Miss Greer might have waited in the treatment room being systematically ignored till the cows came home.

"We need to get some X-rays," the young doctor declared. "You two can wait out front."

Reece wasn't good at waiting, she soon discovered. He spent a lot of time outside the hospital's glass doors, pacing and talking on his cell phone. He looked at his watch a lot.

Sara didn't even wear a watch. If she needed to know the time, she could look at her cell phone—if it was charged.

At one point Reece disappeared, but when he came back he brought her an apple and a cup of coffee from the cafeteria. A peace offering, perhaps? Or maybe he just didn't want her passing out from hunger.

Finally a nurse called them back. Miss Greer had been returned to her treatment room, looking none too happy. A doctor was waiting for them—a different one.

"Your grandmother's hip is broken," he said matter-of-factly. "The joint was in bad shape to begin with. If she wants to walk again, we'll have to replace the hip."

"She's not our—" Sara started to say, but Reece nudged her with his elbow. She cleared her throat. "Then of course she should have the surgery. Right, Grandma?"

"I told the doctor just to give me some crutches and let me go home," Miss Greer grumbled, "but he doesn't listen."

"How long will she be in the hospital?" Reece asked.

"Given her age, at least a few days. But once she's home, she'll need a lot of help. We'll assign a home-health aide and a physical therapist, but she still can't stay alone—not for at least a month."

"She has me," Sara said. "I live with her."

"I can help, too," Reece said.

"Good. Then you want to proceed with the surgery?"

"Excuse me, Doctor," Miss Greer said, "it's my hip that's broken, not my brain. Stop talking like I can't hear you."

Sara bit her lip. It was refreshing to hear her landlady giving someone besides her an earful, for a change. "Grandma, you want the surgery, right?"

"No, but if there's no other way to get better, I guess I'll have to do it." She looked at her own watch. "Oh, Holy Ghost, the guests will be arriving any minute and no one is there to greet them."

"They'll let themselves in," Sara said reassuringly.

An orderly came to transfer Miss Greer to a room, leaving Sara and Reece standing alone in the hallway. She looked at him, eyes full of worry. "Why don't you go back to the Sunsetter? I want to stay for a while longer and make sure she's taken care of."

"How will you get home?"

She shrugged. "Oh, I'll find a way, I always do."

Reece could just imagine. Would she hitchhike? Take a bus? "What if I come back in a while to get you?"

"That's a lot of driving."

"It's only forty minutes. I don't mind." He really didn't mind. The woman was exciting to be around, even if she did keep him in a constant state of semi-arousal. Anyway, what else did he have to do?

He had already set up the bookkeeping for Remington Charters, the business he and his cousins had inherited from their uncle. He could have gone home a week ago, and really he should have. But he'd been dragging his feet, pretending there was more work to do, and not quite sure why. For the first time in his life he wasn't eager to return to his office and the numbers he loved.

Numbers were reliable. He understood them. He could rely on them to behave. Beautiful, wild, chestnut-haired women, on the other hand, were a complete mystery to him.

But he now realized Sara was at least part of the reason he hadn't rushed home to his job, although she clearly was a most unsuitable woman for him.

Relationships were all about compatibility. Having the same interests, the same values. The fact that she got his juices flowing simply wasn't enough.

"Well, if you really don't mind driving all that way," Sara said, "I'd appreciate it. Miss Greer will rest easier knowing someone is looking after the guests."

"What rooms should I put them in?" Reece asked.

"The Silversteins always like the Orchid Room...no, wait, maybe that's the Canfields who like to stay there. They're coming next week...or the week after. But for sure, put the Taylors in the Tea Rose...or maybe it's the Lilac Room." She waved a dismissive hand. "It's in the calendar at the front desk."

Miss Greer wasn't kidding about Sara being bad with the details. She was intelligent and well-read. He'd often seen her tucked into the window seat in the side parlor, reading something really dense like Proust or Hemingway.

Yet she was a disaster when it came to numbers and details. Why was that?

"I should go," Reece said. "I'll come back around eight o'clock. We can grab a bite afterward, if you want to." He held his breath. Had he actually just invited Sara Kaufman to have dinner with him?

She surprised him with a warm smile. "I'd like that. Ooh, I heard about this great restaurant not too far from here. I've been dying to try it."

"Okay, sounds good." And it saved him the agony of coming up with some place to take her that she would enjoy.

SARA WAS WAITING in front of the hospital when Reece pulled up precisely at eight o'clock. She waved and trotted toward the car, jumping into the passenger seat. The car suddenly seemed a more cheerful place, filled with her colors and the scents of vanilla and cinnamon that swirled around her wherever she went.

She looked a little tired, but as usual she was smiling. "Right on time."

"I hate being late." Besides, he was hungry. He usually ate dinner early, went to bed early, woke up early. He liked getting to the office before anyone else, when he could really concentrate in the quiet. Just him and the numbers.

"Did you get the guests checked in?" Sara asked.

He nodded. "When I got back I found the Silversteins roaming about the living room a little puzzled by the fact no one was there to greet them. But when I explained about Miss Greer's accident, they were completely understanding. The other two couples arrived right after. I got them all settled into their rooms."

Then, because he'd promised Miss Greer, he'd listened to messages, returned phone calls and taken three reservations. Business was certainly heating up as summer approached.

"How is Miss Greer?" he asked as he pulled away from the curb without any clue where they were going.

"Resting comfortably. She's scheduled for surgery first thing in the morning. Meanwhile, they gave her some pain meds that worked pretty well, though they made her a little bit loopy."

"Loopy?" That was hard to imagine.

"She thought she was a little girl, and she spoke in German. Did you know she came over from Germany right after the war?"

"I truthfully don't know anything about Miss Greer. She's not exactly chatty."

"Sometimes when she's baking, she'll let things slip."

"Speaking of baking…" Reece said, "I assume you'll want to be at the hospital for Miss Greer's surgery tomorrow."

"Yes, of course," Sara said passionately. "Someone has to be here for her. But what does that have to do with baking?"

"What about breakfast?"

"I can grab something here." Then she gasped. "Oh, my gosh, who's going to feed the guests?"

Exactly what Reece was wondering.

Sara looked at him, her eyes beseeching. "I don't suppose you'd—"

"Oh, no. I don't even know how the coffeemaker works. Where are we going, by the way?"

She looked around, orienting herself. "Turn right at the light. Reece, you *have* to do breakfast. It's easy. I'll get everything ready for you. All you have to do is pull things out of the oven. Then there's just the easy stuff—orange juice, yogurt, toast—oh, shoot, I need to bake bread, too." She looked at her watch. "Maybe we shouldn't do dinner after all."

Reece was surprised at how disappointed he felt. He *wanted* to take Sara to dinner. "I'll help," he said. "I guess if I don't actually have to cook, I can handle it. As soon as we're done with dinner, we'll go back and I'll help you all I can to get ready for tomorrow."

Her smile lit up the whole car. "Great."

Yeah, great. He wondered if he should refund the Silversteins and the others some of their money. Part of the appeal of a B and B was a fancy, fabulous breakfast. But with Reece in charge, he was afraid it would be distinctly non-fabulous. He would shoot for edible.

"Just so you know, cooking was the one Boy Scout badge I never got. And I made it to Eagle Scout."

"You were a Boy Scout? That's so cute."

Cute? He didn't want Sara to think of him as "cute." But he supposed "hot and studly" was out of the question.

"Sara, where are we going again?"

She looked around. "Oh, shoot. I forgot to tell you to turn at the last light."

"No problem." Reece made a U-turn. "So where is it?"

"I'm not sure of the exact address, but I think I know how to get there."

"And what's this place called?"

"I don't remember, exactly. But I think it's an Indian place. Or maybe Pakistani. Maybe there's an elephant on the sign."

Pakistani food? No, thanks. Despite the fact New York had ethnic restaurants on every corner, he was a meat-and-potatoes man. Spicy, foreign food had never done anything but give him heartburn. He didn't even like pepperoni on his pizza.

Well, maybe he could get a hamburger. Few restaurants would refuse to cook a hamburger.

"I think you turn left at this next light," Sara said uncertainly.

"You think?"

"It's around here somewhere, don't worry."

Easy for her to say, but he hated not knowing where he was. It would never occur to him to wander around until he found a restaurant that he sort of knew the location of. If he'd been the one planning dinner, he would have found the name and address of the restaurant, programmed the information into his satellite navigation system and followed the directions.

"Want to look at the map?" He pointed to his GPS, which showed their current location.

"Oh, I can't make heads or tails of maps. It's easier for me to find things by feel."

They wandered around for another fifteen minutes, making what Reece knew were increasingly random turns, until it became clear they were hopelessly lost.

"I saw a steak house back that way," Reece said. "We could try that."

Sara wrinkled her nose. "Steak is so boring. I know I can find this place. Give me five more minutes."

In five more minutes he was going to start eating the leather on the dashboard. But he obliged her and, miracle of miracles, after a couple more turns, they found themselves at a strip shopping center in the middle of which was a sign with a red goat on it. The restaurant was called Sofia, and it was neither Indian nor Pakistani, but Bulgarian.

"That's it!" Sara cried triumphantly. "I told you I could find it."

"If we drove every street in Corpus Christi, we'd find it by process of elimination," he grumbled. "Anyway, I don't see an elephant."

She punched him lightly on the arm. "Don't be a spoilsport. We're here, aren't we? And that goat *looks* like an elephant."

They were somewhere. Which was not cause for celebration as far as Reece was concerned. He would've preferred the steak house. Yes, he was set in his ways. But he liked his ways.

"I'm not eating goat meat," he said, though he did pull into a parking place. He could at least give the place a try, since Sara seemed to be so excited about it.

"You've never eaten goat?"

He pulled a face. "Have you?"

"Sure. In Mexico, *cabrito* is served everywhere. It's good."

"It's *goat* meat."

"Well, I'm sure this place serves something you'll like."

The restaurant was kind of interesting, he had to admit, reminding him of something you might find in the Village. The décor was dark and red and suitably exotic, and everyone who worked there appeared to be actually from Bulgaria. The mouthwatering smell of grilled meats made Reece's stomach growl. Maybe this wouldn't be so horrible after all.

The prices were certainly reasonable. Not that he minded paying premium prices for really good food.

Sara ordered Bulgarian red wine, cold cucumber-yogurt soup, and some kind of pepper stuffed with meat and rice.

"Do you have a hamburger?" Reece asked when the waiter turned to him. "Or a plain beef steak?"

Sara and the waiter wore twin expressions of horror.

"Reece," Sara said, "you can't come to a restaurant like this and order hamburger. I'm not sure they even serve beef here. Don't you want to try something interesting?"

"I don't really like spicy food," he said, feeling boring all of a sudden.

"How about this?" Sara asked, pointing to an unpronounceable word on the menu. "It's supposed to be like a shepherd's pie."

That didn't sound so bad. "Okay."

Sara smiled, pleased, and Reece suddenly realized he would eat just about anything—even goat—to get that smile.

"Spicy food is an acquired taste," she said when the waiter had gone. "If you experiment, you'll find things you like."

"I might like it, but my ulcer wouldn't."

"Ulcer? You have an ulcer?"

"I did two years ago." It was the most miserable experience of his entire life. "Don't worry, it's better now. But I try not to tempt fate by eating weird stuff."

"Hmm. I'll bet your ulcer had a lot more to do with your work than your diet."

His doctor had shared that opinion, but he'd refused to believe it. "Not likely. I love my work."

"You eat, drink and sleep your work," she countered. "You always have your cell phone glued to your ear, or your nose against the screen of your laptop. You check your watch constantly."

He shrugged. "Unfortunately, my department doesn't run itself."

Sara's observations weren't new to him. He knew he spent more time and energy on his work than was strictly healthy.

He'd thought everything was under control in his

department when he'd left almost a month ago for what was supposed to be a two-week leave of absence.

But the job had escalated when ownership of the business came into dispute, and the eventual resolution involved a complex merger of interests among the Remington cousins and Cooper's soon-to-be wife, Allie Bateman.

Problems had also cropped up at his regular job, problems only he could solve.

"Did I say something wrong?" Sara said. "You suddenly got this look on your face like you swallowed a bug."

He shook off his dismal thoughts. Tonight, at least, he ought to be able to forget about his job. He forced a smile. "No, you didn't say anything wrong. You're right, I do work too hard. But that's the nature of the beast."

When their dinners arrived, Reece was pleasantly surprised. His shepherd's pie was delicious, flavored with a delicate blend of seasonings that weren't at all hot as he'd anticipated. He did pick out a few suspiciously unidentifiable purple things, but other than that it was fine.

He declined dessert, but Sara ordered a gooey pastry, and he thoroughly enjoyed watching her eat it. She did so with gusto, relishing every bite with her eyes closed.

After watching her lush lips close around the fork a few times, however, he started thinking about things he shouldn't, and he had to force himself to look away.

"Let me pay it," Sara said when the check arrived. "I'm the one who ate a lot."

"Don't be ridiculous." He snatched the bill from her hand. "Dinner was my idea." And he knew she didn't have a lot of disposable income. Although her room and board were taken care of, her various temporary and part-time jobs couldn't net all that much extra cash.

"Let me at least leave the tip." She reached into her big straw bag and pulled out what could only be described as a money ball. She peeled a few ones from it and set them on the table, then dropped the rest back into her bag.

"You don't have to—"

"It's done."

He didn't want to argue with her, but it seemed less like a date if he let her pay even a small amount. Maybe that was her true purpose. Maybe she wanted to subtly let him know that just because they'd shared dinner, he shouldn't have any expectations.

Of course he didn't. Sara was as friendly as a puppy, but that didn't mean she had any designs on—or interest in—his person.

When they returned to the B and B, they went immediately to the kitchen, where Reece got a taste of just how much work a gourmet breakfast required. Sara had made it look easy—almost effortless—in the past as she'd delivered plate after plate to the dining room. But Reece had never ventured into the kitchen during the preparations.

First Sara made up the dough for two loaves of bread.

"It's quick bread," she explained, "so it doesn't require a lot of rising time." She popped it into the oven, then went to work making up the batter for blueberry and cranberry muffins.

He remembered when he was a kid his mom had occasionally made muffins from a box, but this was altogether more complex, with lots of chopping and folding.

Sara let Reece chop nuts—for a few minutes, anyway.

"Good Lord, you're going to lop off a finger using a knife that way!" She took the knife away from him. "Here, why don't you whip some eggs for the frittata."

"The fri-what?"

It turned out "frittata" was just a fancy name for eggs and fresh vegetables, bacon, cheese and spices. When the eggs were whipped, Sara put Reece to work grating cheese, a job he couldn't mess up too badly except when he grated his knuckles.

She sliced fresh strawberries and added sugar. By now she was out of jobs he could do, so he just watched. Her hands were small, quick and clever. The knife moved so fast it was a blur. Most interesting was her face. As she worked, she wore an expression of such contentment and serenity he thought she looked like an angel.

A mischievous angel, maybe, with that halo of brown curls around her face and the smudge of flour on her cheek.

"The fruit is in case anyone wants cereal or oatmeal, which they usually don't."

"Oatmeal?"

She laughed. "Oh, now surely you can make oatmeal. You eat it every morning."

He shook his head. "Honestly, I don't cook. Nothing."

She sighed. "Don't offer oatmeal, then."

When they were finally finished, it was close to

midnight. They tidied up the kitchen and turned out the light.

The bulb popped just as Sara switched it off, and they were plunged into darkness.

"Oh, hang it, that lightbulb burns out all the time," Sara said, her voice coming to him soft and velvety in the dark, sending a pleasurable chill up his spine.

"I'll change it tomorrow morning," Reece said. "Let's not worry about it now."

"Yeah, but what happened to the lamp in the living room? It's on a timer, and it always comes on at night."

"I'll check it tomorrow, too." But for now he would enjoy the darkness. It seemed so…sexy.

"But I can't see."

"Hold on to me. I can see well enough." As his eyes adjusted, he could make out the outlines of furniture and pictures on the wall.

She grabbed on to his arm. "What are you, a bat? It's pitch-dark in here."

"Men have better night vision than women. On average," he added as they made their way slowly through the dining room to the living room. After hours of feeling like an idiot in the kitchen, Reece was pleased to be in charge of something, even if it was only navigating them through a dark house.

"Is that true?" she asked, sounding genuinely curious.

"I read it somewhere. It must be true."

Halfway up the stairs, light from the upstairs landing illuminated the steps. But Sara didn't let go of his arm. They'd created a bond, caring for Miss Greer, sharing the adventurous dinner, then working together in the kitchen. He felt close to her in a way he hadn't felt close to a woman in a long time, and it was nice.

Very, very nice.

They paused in front of Reece's bedroom door, and she still didn't let him go. He grabbed the opportunity with both hands.

"Sara, I just want you to know that I admire the way you took care of Miss Greer and volunteered to handle things for her. Not everyone would be that generous."

She smiled up at him. "Miss Greer has been kind to me. I know she's a little bit gruff and abrupt, sometimes, but she really does love me like a granddaughter. The B and B is my home, and we take care of each other."

"What about your family?"

"My parents aren't exactly the nurturing kind. They're both military—spit 'n' polish, no crying allowed, pull yourself up by your bootstraps. I don't ask them for help and they don't offer."

"Where do they live?"

"At MacShane—you know, the army base about fifty miles inland?"

Reece nodded. He'd seen it on a map, but that was about it.

"I'm not a military brat in the usual sense, though," she said. "They didn't move around. Both of them spent almost their entire careers at MacShane. Don't get me wrong, they're good people and they were good parents. But I'm so different from them. They don't get me and I don't get them, but we love each other in our own ways."

Reece understood growing up with less-than-warm-and-fuzzy parents. His were rigid, also, especially with him. Whatever nurturing instincts they had got used up on his older brother, Bret.

"I don't exactly get you, either," he said. "But I think you're…unique."

She wrinkled her nose. "Unique? Is that the best you can do, Reece Remington?"

All right, so sweet-talking women had never been his strong suit. He possessed other good qualities. Like kissing. He'd been told he was a very good kisser.

Before he could chicken out, he pulled off his glasses, slipped his arms around her and brought his mouth to hers.

Chapter Three

Sara sank into the kiss, which was like melted butter on a warm biscuit—better than she could have dreamed. His mouth was demanding but somehow gentle as he coaxed her lips open, one hand buried in the hair at the back of her neck, angling her head just how he wanted it.

He teased her upper lip with his tongue, then did the same with her lower lip. She entwined her arms around his neck, at first to draw closer, then to keep from sinking to the floor as her knees turned to jelly and she lost all feeling in her extremities.

The kiss seemed to go on forever as their tongues met and performed a mating dance. It was, hands down, the sexiest, most provocative kiss she'd ever experienced, and she loved it that he didn't immediately press for more. He didn't touch her breasts, he didn't grind his pelvis into hers.

He just kissed her like it was the last kiss either of them would ever have. Oh, God, she hoped not.

Finally he pulled back and looked down at her, faintly amused. "Unique, and you have really soft lips."

"O-okay, that's better."

"Go get some sleep. We have a busy day ahead of us." He released her, brushing his lips against her forehead before disappearing into his room.

Huh. She wanted so badly to go in there with him. But he hadn't invited her.

She headed for the attic stairs that led to her bedroom, but her legs refused to carry her up them, and she sank onto the second step and stared at Reece's door.

Wow. That had been a surprise.

Maybe she should have forced him out of his comfort zone sooner. Certainly that Bulgarian restaurant hadn't been a comfortable place for him. Neither had he felt at home in the B and B's kitchen. He'd bungled around like…well, like a macho man in a kitchen.

She'd been surprised each time he'd risen to her challenges. He'd tried the slightly strange food. He'd allowed her to show him things in the kitchen.

And then he'd kissed her. Connection?

The only problem was, what was she going to do now? Had she started something she wasn't prepared to finish?

She used to take romance lightly, easy come, easy go. If a relationship didn't work out, she might be sad for a short time, but there were always new men to be found.

Recently, however, she'd been wondering whether she had a soul mate out there. Allie, who only a few weeks ago had been confirmedly single, had found love with Cooper Remington, and Sara had begun to feel left out.

But if she were to "settle down," it would take a special kind of guy, one who was as adventurous as she was, who loved traveling and trying new things.

She had to admit, Reece didn't strike her as the least bit adventurous. He was ultraserious, a buttoned-down CPA who loved to talk about risk management and long-term projections.

Her projections usually didn't extend past what she planned to have for lunch that day.

And yet…he was so delicious. Not only that, but he was a good guy. He hadn't balked—not really—when she'd volunteered him to handle the B and B finances while Miss Greer took care of her health. Delicious men came and went, but ones with character—they were a bit more rare.

Maybe she ought to decide what she wanted from Reece before she did something crazy.

SARA WAS UP before light the next day, but when she reached the kitchen, she found Reece already there, pondering the workings of the coffeemaker. She liked seeing him there. His very male presence balanced all the Victorian froufrou.

"You already changed the lightbulbs?" she asked, instead of saying good morning.

He jumped. "Oh. Yeah." He looked everywhere but at her.

He was probably regretting last night's moment of weakness. Fine. If that was how he wanted to play it, she could pretend it never happened. "I'll get the coffee ready. You can preheat the upper oven to three hundred ten degrees, and the lower one to four twenty-five."

"Okay."

That took him all of twenty seconds. When he was

done, he intently watched her make coffee, as if committing every step to memory. His attention, so focused, gave her a delicate shiver.

"Are you cold?" he asked. "I opened the window when I came down because it seemed stuffy, but I can close it."

"No, the fresh air is nice." She chuckled. "I'm surprised you were able to get the window open at all. Miss Greer has a phobia about fresh air. Even in the dead of summer, she's sure everyone will catch their death of cold if there's a draft."

"Well, Miss Greer isn't here, and what she doesn't know won't hurt her."

Sara's heart thudded hard as she chanced a look over her shoulder at Reece. His brown eyes sparkled with mischief. Was he trying to tell her something else? Did he know that she'd been holding back a bit because he was a guest, and hitting on guests was frowned upon?

Now that Reece was sort of part of the management, did that change everything?

She looked away quickly, wondering if it was too late to undo last night's kiss. For the first time in her life, she was a bit scared of getting involved on any level with a man, and she wasn't quite sure why. Would she get out unscathed if she and Reece got carried away with this attraction thing?

He was just so different from the guys she usually went for, and she felt she didn't know the rules anymore.

"Why don't you set the table?" she suggested brightly. "Linens are in the buffet, dishes in the china cabinet. Set six place settings."

"What about me?" he asked. "Don't I get to eat?"

"You're the hired help now. We eat in the kitchen."

"I don't see how I can be hired help if I'm not getting paid," he pointed out good-naturedly, though he moved to the dining room to follow directions.

She pushed the coffeemaker's on button as she realized what he said was perfectly true. She was getting free room and board, but no one had promised Reece a similar deal for helping out.

She poked her head through the doorway. "You're absolutely right. But I'm sure Miss Greer doesn't expect you to pay full price for staying here when you're running the place."

Reece shook his head as he took out a floral tablecloth and laid it over the huge mahogany dining table. "I was only kidding. I don't need to be paid. I don't mind helping out, and it gives me something to do."

"Don't you have to work on the accounting for Remington Charters?" Sara asked.

"Well, yeah, but that's not exactly a full-time job."

"I thought you'd be done with all that by now." She helped him straighten the cloth, then dug out coordinating place mats while he grabbed a stack of plates from the china cabinet.

"I have a few more things to set up, then I have to train Allie and Cooper how to use the program."

"Train Allie, you mean," she said. "Cooper doesn't have the patience for dealing with numbers."

Reece looked at her quizzically. "That's true, but how did you know that?"

"Duh. You guys lived here for more than a week

before Cooper and Max found their own places. I observed you. I watched conversations. I can tell you a lot about your cousins."

Reece crossed his arms. "You eavesdropped?"

"Absolutely not." She hoped she wasn't blushing. Maybe she'd listened to Reece more than was strictly accidental because of her fascination with him. "Hired help is often invisible. People talk as if I'm not there, though I make no effort to sneak around. Sometimes I can't help overhearing."

"You weren't invisible to me."

"Ha. When you have your nose in your laptop with some accounting program, you wouldn't notice an atomic blast going off in the next room. I used to vacuum right under your chair and you never twitched."

"I did notice," he insisted. "I noticed lots of things about you."

"Like what?"

"Like some guy named Ike from Santa Fe called you at least three times a day on your cell phone. You didn't want to encourage him, but you didn't want to hurt his feelings, either."

She blinked in surprise. "Now who's eavesdropping?"

"Sometimes I couldn't help overhearing," he said, echoing exactly what she'd just said to him.

Gracious. He wasn't nearly as oblivious as she'd guessed. Here she thought she hadn't even registered on his radar, and he'd been listening to her conversations.

"What else do you know about Cooper?" he asked.

"Aren't you more curious as to how much I know about you?"

He looked away. "I don't give off that many clues."

"You're thirty-four years old. You're the youngest of two brothers, your brother is named Bret, and he dumps a lot of work on you."

Reece opened his mouth, but no words came out.

"You've never been married," she continued. That was more of an educated guess than actual knowledge, but she could see the moment she said it that it was true, and she felt unaccountably relieved. "Bret is already married and has two kids, a boy and a girl…Bret Jr. and Jessica."

"Not bad."

"You like things neat, and you make your bed every morning even though that's my job. You get seasick and you have seasonal allergies."

"How do you know that?"

"I'm the maid. I clean your bathroom and I've seen the medicine you leave out on the counter."

"You're a snoop!" But he softened the comment with a smile. "I bet you wouldn't want some man looking at *your* private things."

She shrugged. "You can look in my bathroom any time you want. Especially if you're willing to scrub the toilet." He wouldn't find anything shocking. The most controversial thing in her medicine chest were birth control pills, which she often forgot to take because lately there hadn't been any compelling reason to. She and Ike hadn't made it that far because she'd quickly realized he wasn't for her.

He'd finally gotten the message, too, thank God.

The antique clock on the buffet chimed the half hour, and Sara realized she needed to get a move on. "The frittata comes out of the oven at six-fifty," she said.

"The muffins, in about five minutes. You'll need to make the orange juice from frozen—we don't have any fresh oranges today, but I'll stop at the grocery on my way home. Is there anything else you need to know?"

"Um, Sara?"

"Yes?"

"How were you planning to get to the hospital?"

Oh, damn. The automotive fairies hadn't magically materialized a new car for her last night. She gave Reece a beseeching look. "You won't let me borrow yours?"

His expression told her exactly what he thought of that idea. Some men were a little funny about loaning out their cars, and she didn't really blame him, since the Mercedes was so new.

"Miss Greer needs me," she said. "I'm a very good driver. I'll drive like my grandmother, I swear."

He wavered, then finally, looking resigned, reached into his jeans pocket and pulled out a set of keys.

She took them, then impulsively threw her arms around him and kissed him—on the cheek at the last minute instead of his mouth, since another kiss like last night's was apt to addle her brains so thoroughly she would drive into a lamppost.

"Thanks, Reece, you're a peach. If you need anything, my cell number is stuck to the fridge."

"Tell Miss Greer I hope she's better soon."

"I will. Bye!" She got out of there before he had a chance to change his mind.

REECE PEEKED out the lace curtains at the front windows and watched as Sara jumped into his car, gunned the motor and sped off, gravel flying. She hadn't taken the time to adjust the seat or the mirrors.

Too bad he couldn't call the Department of Motor Vehicles and check her driving record, but he had a sneaking feeling that being a "good driver" was all in Sara's mind.

He had no more time to think about his poor car, though. Breakfast called. He remembered the muffins just in time. While they cooled he mixed up some frozen orange juice—luckily the instructions were on the can.

Then it was time to take out the frittata, which he had to admit smelled pretty good. But those little bits of green and red floating around in the eggs were peppers, and peppers were scary.

He poured himself some coffee, then remembered he wasn't supposed to drink it on an empty stomach, so he located last night's bread. The golden loaves made his mouth water, but they were unsliced.

He got out a cutting board and bread knife—at least, he was pretty sure it was a bread knife—and started slicing. But his slices were thick and ungainly, nothing like the thin, regular slices he was used to seeing at the Sunsetter's breakfast table.

The first guests arrived for breakfast right at seven. The Taylors were a young couple who were planning to visit the nearby wildlife refuge.

Reece brought out the coffeepot. "Breakfast will be ready shortly," he said as he poured the husband's coffee. But the wife stopped him.

"I'd like hot tea, please."

"Tea." Sara hadn't mentioned anything about tea. "Coming right up."

"And do you have skim milk for the coffee?" the husband asked.

Blech. "I'll check."

Tea required boiling water. A kettle sat on the stove, so Reece filled it and turned on the burner. He found a carton of skim milk in the fridge and started to bring it out to the dining room, but he remembered that both Sara and Miss Greer always put everything in nice dishes. He had to rummage for a cream pitcher.

Then the water was boiling. Oh, God, what should he do with it? Where were the tea bags?

The toast popped up, but he didn't have time to eat it. He put in more of his lumpy, uneven slices for the guests, brought the whole kettle to the dining room and poured it into Mrs. Taylor's cup as she looked on, puzzled.

"I suppose you'd like a tea bag," he said.

Mrs. Taylor pointed at the buffet. "They're right there." Thank God.

He brought out the frittata just as the second couple, the Silversteins, arrived. They, of course, wanted coffee right away, but with half-and-half, not skim milk.

"Could we get something to serve the frittata?" Mr. Taylor asked, when Reece returned with the half-and-half carton—he couldn't find another cream pitcher, though he knew there must be one somewhere.

"Just scoop it up with your hands," Reece said in a lame attempt at humor. When no one laughed, he retreated, found a spatula, and brought it to Mr. Taylor.

The third couple, the Benedicts, arrived. They were

elderly, and Mr. Benedict started clamoring for prune juice.

Reece realized he hadn't offered any of them juice. The toast had popped up and was getting cold.

He found the prune juice, poured orange juice, buttered toast and set it on the table. Someone asked for jam, and he had to find all the different flavored jams, put them in jam pots as he'd seen Sara and Miss Greer do a dozen times, and set them out.

Coffee refills. Juice refills. The muffins! He'd forgotten all about them. It took him precious time to find a basket and a cloth to line it with. He dumped the muffins into the basket and set it on the table.

"Do you have any yogurt?" Mrs. Silverstein asked.

"What about oatmeal?" Mr. Benedict asked. "Don't you usually serve oatmeal with fresh strawberries?"

"No oatmeal today," Reece said apologetically. "Miss Greer is having surgery this morning and Sara, her helper, is with her. I'm doing the best I can, but I know it's not what you're used to."

"As long as you don't serve us those cream puffs," Mrs. Silverstein said with a sniff. The cream puffs were Miss Greer's specialty, and everyone despised them, though no one had the heart to tell her they weren't very good.

By the time the guests had eaten their fill and left the table, Reece was exhausted, his stomach burned, and he had a whole new respect for Sara's skills.

Well, okay, she did have an alarming tendency to spill things on *him*, but other than that, cooking and serving breakfast appeared as effortless as breathing to Sara.

He still had a lot of work ahead of him, he realized. The dining room looked like the cafeteria scene from *Animal House.*

He'd just started stacking dishes to carry into the kitchen when the phone rang. He went to answer it. "Hello? I mean, Sunsetter Bed-and-Breakfast, can I help you?"

"It's me, Sara."

Reece was amazed at the rush of relief and pleasure he got from just the sound of her voice. "Hey, Sara. Is everything all right?"

"Miss Greer just got out of surgery, and the doctor said it went fine. She's in recovery. It looks like I'll be here a while longer, though."

"No need to hurry home," he said. "I have everything under control."

"Really?"

"You sound surprised."

"I didn't peg you for the domestic type."

"Nothing to it," he said as he wedged the phone under his chin and started shoving dishes into the industrial-size dishwasher. "Did you have any trouble with the car?"

She greeted his question with a long silence.

"Sara?"

"Define trouble."

Reece's stomach renewed its churning. "Sara, what happened to my car?"

"Miss Greer is waking up now, I have to go. Bye!"

Chapter Four

Sara disconnected the phone, her heart pounding. She'd only delayed the inevitable; sooner or later she would have to tell Reece she'd had a wreck in his car.

It was just a minor fender bender, and not her fault, either. She'd been innocently looking for a parking space, and another car had backed right into her. But since she'd been in a hurry, and both cars were drivable, she'd quickly exchanged information with the other driver and gone on about her business.

Reece's previously pristine car was now caved in on the right side, the passenger door inoperable.

Well, Reece would just have to understand. It could have happened to anyone, and the important thing was that no one was hurt.

She hoped he would see it that way.

Sara dropped her cell phone into her bag and went back inside to check on Miss Greer. She didn't know if the older woman was waking up yet or not, but she *might* be. She really ought not to have fibbed to Reece, though. That was a bad habit, telling little white lies. As her father always said, a lie was a lie and the size was immaterial.

Miss Greer woke a short time later, but she was in a lot of pain. Sara spent the rest of the morning tracking down a doctor who could prescribe something that would make the poor woman more comfortable, then hanging around to make sure the nurses gave it to her. After that, when Miss Greer's lunch was delivered, Sara had to coax the elderly woman to eat a few bites.

It was something of a full-time job, making sure Miss Greer got the care she needed. By the time she was fully awake, adequately fed and reasonably pain-free all at the same time, it was almost dark.

Sara probably should have checked in with Reece again, but she'd aggressively put him out of her mind while she kept busy with Miss Greer. She hoped he was getting along all right taking care of the guests; he'd sounded okay earlier. Breakfast was the hardest part; she was sure he could make up beds and run the vacuum.

Although, come to think of it, she hadn't reminded him he needed to do those things. Since he'd been a guest for some time, he probably knew the drill. But men were a little dense when it came to housework. Some she'd known obviously thought the elves came in at night and cleaned.

It was almost dark by the time she pulled Reece's Mercedes onto Magnolia Street and parked it across the road from the Sunsetter, close to some bushes. Maybe the damage wouldn't look so bad in the dark. Reece wasn't an excitable type; he would probably be calm and reasonable about the whole thing.

Her hopes were dashed when she spotted him pacing on the front porch, his cell phone glued to his ear.

He saw her then and snapped his phone shut. He had started toward her as she got out of the car, and she quavered a bit at the thunderous expression on his face.

"Sara, where have you been? I've been worried sick about you. I've been calling your cell phone all day."

"I can't keep it turned on inside the hospital," she reminded him.

He stopped inches from her and placed his fists on his lean hips. "You couldn't check your messages every once in a while?"

"Sorry. I guess I was pretty focused on taking care of Miss Greer." Yeah, right. She was such a saint. She'd deliberately left her phone off because she knew Reece would be frantic about his car.

"So what happened to the car?" he asked, finally taking his laserlike gaze off her and aiming it at the Mercedes.

"I had a—" she swallowed, her mouth feeling as if it was full of shredded wheat "—a small accident."

"Accident?"

"Just a small one."

Reece eyed the car from bumper to bumper and, apparently seeing no damage, walked around to the other side.

Sara knew the moment he saw the crunched-in door. She longed to flee to the safety of her room, where she wouldn't have to endure his anger. But one thing her parents had taught her—and that had sunk in—was that she had to take responsibility for her actions.

"How did this happen?"

"Someone backed into me in the parking lot."

A muscle twitched in his jaw. "So it wasn't your fault?"

She shook her head. "The guy apologized all over the place."

"You have a police report?"

Again she shook her head. "We exchanged information." She reached into her bag and pulled out a rumpled piece of paper onto which she'd written the man's name, phone number and driver's license number.

Reece walked back around to the street and took the paper from her. He examined it briefly before meticulously creasing it and placing it in his wallet. "I can't believe you wrecked my new car."

"It wasn't my fault."

"Maybe not technically, but you drive like you do everything else."

"What's that supposed to mean?"

"Full throttle, damn the consequences."

He turned and walked back into the house without a backward glance.

His attack was so unfair, and his harsh judgment cut her to the bone. But Sara resisted the juvenile urge to cry. She'd learned not to. When she was little, and her father yelled at her for some sin, real or imagined, she couldn't help the tears. But crying only made everything worse. If she cried, her father would just scold her for crying, too. He'd told her not to be a crybaby.

Reece was not her father, she reminded herself. But she didn't like this self-righteous side of him.

He hadn't even tried to listen or show some understanding. He'd gotten in the last word and walked away.

Now they had this thing between them.

Realizing she couldn't stand in the street forever, she moved her leaden feet toward the front porch. This hadn't been the best day of her life, but neither had it been the worst. Stuff happened. She would go into the kitchen, fix up a nice soup and maybe even show Reece she was a bigger person than he was by offering to share. Then she would get everything ready for breakfast tomorrow. She would have to return to the hospital tomorrow morning to make sure Miss Greer was doing okay, but she could wait until after breakfast was served.

She had no idea how she would get to Corpus Christi, but she would figure something out. Maybe Allie would loan Sara her car. She seldom needed it during the day, when she was out on her boat running one of her charter trips.

The B and B guests were all in the living room when Sara entered the house, drinking cocktails and talking about where they would have dinner that night.

Had Reece served them the wine? Miss Greer kept a few bottles of inexpensive wine around, usually to serve the guests on their first night at the B and B.

"Oh, Sara," said Mrs. Silverstein, who had stayed at the Sunsetter many times, "how is Miss Greer doing?"

"Much better," Sara answered with a smile. "She's looking forward to learning to walk with her new hip."

"I got a new hip last year," said Mrs. Benedict, doing a couple of shallow knee bends to show how flexible she was. "Best thing I ever did for myself. Miss Greer is going to love it!"

Sara felt cheered by the news. Mrs. Benedict was at least as old as Miss Greer, and she was still active. Hopefully Miss Greer still had several good, productive years to look forward to.

"Does anyone need anything before I head to the kitchen?" Sara asked.

The youngest woman in the room, who by process of elimination must be Mrs. Taylor, gave a sultry smile. "Reece has been taking very good care of us."

"Yes," Mrs. Silverstein said. "That new boy you hired is doing very well for himself. The breakfast he served was marvelous!"

Sara stopped herself before she could point out that she was the one who had cooked the breakfast. That would be petty. But it gave her a little pang to realize she could be replaced in the guests' affections so easily.

Sara entered the kitchen expecting it to be a disaster, but Reece had apparently cleaned everything up after breakfast. That was a first. She'd never known a man who would set foot in the kitchen, much less clean it.

Goodness, he'd even run the dishwasher.

She opened the door of the industrial-size dishwasher, pulled out the lower rack intending to put away the dishes, and let out an involuntary shriek.

Miss Greer's beautiful Haviland china looked as if someone had taken a hammer to it.

"What?" Reece appeared in the doorway, out of breath. "What happened?" Then he took in the broken china and his face fell. "Oh, no."

Sara was tempted to tell Reece that any idiot knew not to put fine china into a dishwasher. She experienced a brief, childish urge to make him feel the way he'd made *her* feel not ten minutes ago.

She opened her mouth, then stopped. Truth be known, this was her responsibility. She knew he had little experience in the kitchen. She should have told him those delicate bone china dishes had to be hand washed, especially since this dishwasher was notoriously brutal.

"Can they be fixed?" Reece removed a shard from the dishwasher and examined it. He looked so forlorn, any irritation she'd felt toward him melted away.

"I'm afraid not."

"Were they valuable?"

"Probably only to her. It's her wedding china from her hope chest."

Reece put a hand to his head and leaned against the counter, looking as if someone had just hit him. "God help me. I've destroyed an elderly woman's girlhood dreams. What kind of a monster does that make me?"

"It's not your fault, Reece."

He looked at her, surprised. "You're making me feel worse, you know. You should yell at me."

"I don't want to yell. I don't like yelling."

His guilty expression would have amused her under other circumstances. "I shouldn't have lost my temper about the car. You said it wasn't your fault and I should have accepted that. And even if you were at fault—which I'm sure you weren't—it wouldn't have been on purpose. I'm sorry, Sara."

Now she really wanted to cry. Reece certainly wasn't like her father, who'd never apologized for anything in his life—at least not to her.

"I might have been driving a little fast through the parking lot," she admitted. "Maybe I could have prevented the accident if I'd been more careful. And I should've told you not to put china in the dishwasher. It's my fault, totally. I'll take the blame with Miss Greer."

Reece actually smiled. "Throwing blame around doesn't really make things better, does it? Let's try to solve the problem. Can we replace the dishes?"

Sara relaxed. The hideous "thing" between her and Reece was gone, just with a few words of understanding. Now the dish disaster had been reduced to a tactical challenge, and she liked a good challenge.

"There are services out there that do nothing but sell replacement china, silver and crystal," she said. "But it wouldn't be the same."

"You mean we couldn't match the exact pattern?"

"No, we could probably do that. But they wouldn't be the exact same dishes."

Reece obviously still didn't get it.

"Are you familiar with the concept of sentimental value? These are the very dishes Miss Greer collected, dreaming of a life with a future husband who never materialized. Think how excited she must have been, saving her pennies, buying one plate or saucer at a time, planning for her very first meal. New dishes, even if they looked exactly the same, wouldn't actually *be* the same."

"Could she tell the difference?"

"Are you suggesting we don't tell her?"

"Why break her heart if we don't have to?" Reece countered.

It seemed dishonest, but she supposed Reece had a point.

"All right," Sara agreed reluctantly. "Let's figure out exactly how much is broken so we'll know what pieces to look for."

After removing all of the broken pieces from the dishwasher, they had their tally: three broken dinner plates, two salad plates, six teacups and two saucers. The pattern was Haviland's Tea Rose, according to the seal on the bottom of a plate.

"I'll get started researching this on the Internet," Reece said.

Sara wasn't particularly skilled on the Internet. She didn't even own a computer. "I'll make us some dinner."

"Is that allowed?"

Sara laughed, the first time she'd done so since wrecking Reece's car. Miss Greer was notoriously territorial about the kitchen, and anyone who stayed here any length of time knew it. "She lets me cook for myself," Sara said, "so long as I don't get in her way or smell the place up with onions. But while she's away, we get to make up the rules. I'm going to cook all the things Miss Greer doesn't approve of. Is there anything you especially like to eat?"

He thought for a moment. "Pot roast with potatoes and carrots?"

She should have known. "That's not really my style of cooking. I lean toward vegetarian and ethnic dishes."

"No meat loaf then?"

Honestly, the man had zero imagination when it

came to food. "How about tortilla soup?" she asked. Everyone loved tortilla soup.

Except Reece, apparently. "Look, don't worry about me. I'll go into town to eat."

"Will you at least try what I fix?" she persisted. "It's much more fun to cook for someone other than myself. I mean, restaurant meals are fine, and I love trying new places, but nothing beats a fresh meal from your own kitchen."

"Sure," he said after a very long pause, "but please don't be insulted if I don't eat the spicy stuff."

"I'll tone down the spices just for you." She gave him a little wink, because she couldn't help herself. His life might be boring and predictable, but his food didn't have to be. She was going to convert him to adventurous cuisine if it was her last act on earth.

Chapter Five

Reece's Internet search had started out on an optimistic note.

All of the guests had left for dinner, so Reece had the living room to himself. As he sat on the sofa with his laptop, listening to the comforting clank and clatter of Sara cooking, he discovered a dozen companies that sold replacement china. But he soon found out it wouldn't be as easy as placing the order and waiting for UPS.

Haviland's Pink Tea Rose pattern, he learned, had been produced for only two years, 1955 and 1956, which made it nearly impossible to find. The few pieces that were for sale commanded ridiculous sums. Still, he'd broken the dishes, so he had to replace them. He found four saucers and ordered them; they were sixteen dollars each.

Then he registered with a search service, which would try to find the other pieces he needed. It seemed the sensible thing to do since they would know the best places to look.

Interesting smells began drifting his way from the

kitchen. Miss Greer often fixed herself dinner and, judging from the odor she had favored sausage. This was completely different, and he had to admit it made his mouth water.

Maybe he'd been a little hasty, turning down Sara's cooking.

It was interesting that she was such an enthusiastic cook. Here was a woman who didn't have a home of her own, didn't even own pots and pans, loved traveling. Yet she obviously had a strong streak of domesticity in her.

He felt bad now, getting so aggravated over the damage to his car. He'd already talked to the other driver, who had admitted fault and was willing to have his insurance company handle the whole thing, no arguing.

Maybe Sara could have been more aware of her surroundings, but mistakes happened, as he had so enthusiastically proved with the dishwasher incident. His mother didn't put her china in the dishwasher; he should have known better.

Reece had been accused more than once of expecting a ridiculous degree of perfection from his coworkers— from everyone around him, actually. But his highest standards were reserved for himself. Today had just brought home the fact that nobody was perfect.

"Reece?"

He looked up to see Sara's slim figure silhouetted in the kitchen door. "Yes?"

"I've made soup and sandwiches if you're interested." The uncertainty in her voice pricked his con-

science. For whatever reason, his approval was important to her.

"Sure, sounds good. Let me just finish this one
e-mail." He was in the middle of explaining a complex
financial procedure to his brother, and if he stopped now
he would lose his train of thought completely.

Finishing the message took a bit longer than he
thought it would. It was easy for him to get engrossed
in something and lose track of time. Then he took a
phone call from his father, who wanted to know down
to the second when he would return to the office.

Probably fifteen minutes had passed by the time he
shut down his laptop and headed to the kitchen, but Sara
hadn't nagged him.

He smiled when he saw her, sitting at the small table
in the breakfast nook. She appeared to be sorting
through recipes.

"Sorry that took so long," he said. "I hope the soup
hasn't gotten cold." He had to admit, it smelled pretty
good.

She brightened and set her work aside, shoving it
onto the seat of an empty chair. "No problem. The
longer it simmers, the better it tastes." She bustled
around for a few moments, ladling up soup and slicing
the sandwiches. He enjoyed just watching her perform
everyday tasks.

He used to think she was a bit clumsy. During the first
couple of weeks here she had dropped food on him at least
three times while serving breakfast. But now he could see
that she was actually quite graceful, moving with a beautiful economy, one activity flowing into the next.

Just the same, he tensed as she set his soup in front of him, ready to jump to his feet if the hot liquid appeared to be heading for his lap.

No mishaps today, though.

The meal not only smelled good, it looked beautiful. She'd served the thick ham sandwiches on brown bread with a pickle spear, just like at a restaurant, along with a few tortilla chips. Okay, so he didn't like pickles, and that enormous green thing floating in his soup would have to go. But the effort she'd gone to impressed him.

He tried the sandwich first, because it looked less risky. At his first bite, he realized the bread was rye. He couldn't stand rye bread. And there was something weird on the sandwich, like lettuce but not.

He chewed quickly and swallowed, then washed the bite down with iced tea—sweetened. What was it with Southerners and their tea? Every place he went down here, the tea was so sweet it tasted like syrup.

"The sandwich is made with one of those honey-baked hams," Sara said. "Miss Greer received it as a gift for her birthday last week, but she doesn't care much for it."

"The ham is good," he said without reservation. "What else is on the sandwich?"

"Havarti cheese, brown mustard—oh, and some arugula. I grow it myself in my herb garden on the patio."

"Mmm," he said noncommittally. Had she never heard of American cheese? Regular yellow mustard? Iceberg lettuce? He didn't want to hurt her feelings, but he ought to let her know his preferences. Maybe he would buy some groceries he liked, and she would get the hint.

He ate a few tortilla chips, then went on to brave the soup. Good Lord, what was that *green thing?* He poked at it and discovered it was a slice of avocado. In his opinion, avocados were absolutely the grossest food on earth. Well, next to beets. And asparagus.

He deftly shoved it aside and spooned up some of the broth. Okay, not bad. Kind of strangely spicy. But there was no chicken in the soup. Wasn't tortilla soup supposed to have chicken?

He ate some of the little crunchy things on top and more broth. And when Sara's attention was diverted by her own food, he pulled the ham out of the sandwich, scraped off the mustard, cut it into bites and ate it. Then he put everything else in his napkin, to be disposed of at the first opportunity.

He and his brother had become masters of vegetable disposal from an early age. Their dog, Winston, would eat anything, even broccoli. Unfortunately the Sunsetter didn't have a dog, so he would have to be more creative.

"You don't like avocado?" she asked.

Busted. "It's not my favorite thing," he admitted.

"That's a shame. They're so good for you."

"I thought they were fattening."

"They're high in fat, but it's the good kind of fat."

"I guess I better eat some, then." To appease her, he cut off a tiny piece with his spoon and put it in his mouth, hoping that maybe he was mistaken and it would taste good.

Nope.

He kept eating the broth, but after several spoonfuls

he noticed his tongue was burning. Great. His ulcer was going to love this.

"Thank you for not yelling at me," she said suddenly.

"What? Why would I yell at you?" The dinner wasn't *that* bad.

"When I was sixteen I wrecked my dad's car. It wasn't exactly my fault—a guy pulled out in front of me. But I was so busy trying to look cool that I didn't see him in time."

"Was anyone hurt?" he asked.

"No. The damage wasn't even that bad. But my dad went on and on like I was the stupidest, most irresponsible girl on the face of the earth, and how he knew he shouldn't have let me get my driver's license and how all females and especially teenage girls were bad drivers and on and on and on. He just wouldn't drop it. To this day, if the topic of driving comes up, my dad goes off about how I wrecked the car two weeks after getting my license."

Reece understood demanding parents.

"I guess I'm not the yelling type. Anyway, it's just a car. Easy to fix. It's not like you smashed up a sweet old lady's wedding china."

Sara reached across the table and squeezed his hand. "I'm not the yelling type, either." When she realized her hand was lingering on Reece's arm, she snatched it away and hopped to her feet. "Do you want another sandwich?"

"No, no thanks," he said hastily. "That one was... filling."

"More soup, then?" She cast a critical eye at his bowl, which now contained nothing but soggy onions, celery and tomatoes. "You didn't like the soup."

"Yes, I did. I just ate around a few things that aren't my favorite."

She folded her arms. "You ate the broth."

"And it was very good broth."

"You don't like vegetables of any kind, do you?"

"That's not true. I like green beans. Carrots are okay." He ticked the various items off on his fingers. "Corn. I'll eat corn and...and lettuce. You know, all the normal vegetables. There are just a few I don't like." Okay, more than a few, several of which happened to be in the soup.

She shrugged. "Well, I appreciate that you at least tried the soup. Very adventurous of you."

Hmm, somehow he got the idea she was condescending to him.

THE NEXT MORNING Sara got up early to fix breakfast. She and Reece had decided that he would help her with the meal, then he would visit Miss Greer and stay with her for a while, making sure she got everything she needed.

But it was early yet, and for a few minutes Sara would have the kitchen to herself.

When she opened the lid on the trash to throw away the eggshells, she found something strange. Bread. Cheese. Shriveled leaves of arugula. And a pickle spear.

In short, everything but the ham from Reece's sandwich.

"That little sneak," she muttered. If he didn't like the way she fixed his meals, he needed to tell her rather than wasting perfectly good food.

Honestly, the man was the pickiest eater she'd ever known. Well, no, that title went to her father. He had to have beef and potatoes on the table every night at six-thirty sharp. One or two additional side dishes were tolerated—corn, carrots or an iceberg salad, in rotation.

The first time she'd tasted tacos at a friend's birthday party, she thought she'd landed in a new universe. After that, she had tried every strange new dish she could get her hands on. Once she started experimenting in the kitchen, there'd been no stopping her.

When Reece joined her, she was taking a coffee cake out of the oven.

"That smells fantastic," he said, going straight to the coffeemaker for his morning java fix. Reece did like his coffee, she noticed, and he drank too much of it.

"You don't have to humor me, you know," she said lightly. "If you don't like my cooking, just tell me."

He froze, a guilty expression crossing his handsome face.

"Do you dislike all bread, or just rye?"

"I don't like those seeds," he confessed.

"What about pumpernickel?"

"Not my favorite."

"White?"

He nodded enthusiastically. "White is good."

Figured. He'd probably been raised on Wonder like most American kids and had never branched out.

"I thought maybe I would buy a few groceries today," he said casually. "You shouldn't have to fix all our meals."

"No, please," she said, shuddering at the thought of

what he would bring home. Saltines and cheese from a can? "I like to cook. We'll just have to adjust to each other. But you have to tell me if you don't like something. No more sneaking food into the trash."

"Ah. Now the bread interrogation makes sense." At least he looked a little bit shamed. "I didn't want to hurt your feelings, but it just wasn't my kind of sandwich."

She smiled, suddenly finding the whole situation funny. "Got it."

Reece helped with breakfast as much as he could, but mostly he carried dishes in and out of the dining room and forwarded requests from the guests.

Sara and Reece worked in a comfortable rhythm, which was frankly amazing given that it was only the second breakfast on which they'd cooperated.

Reece, as usual, ate oatmeal. At least that was healthy. But he loaded it with butter and sugar and refused her offer of raisins.

Strawberries. She remembered that he liked strawberries on his oatmeal, and she mentally added them to her grocery list.

She had a sudden vivid memory of wandering through the grocery with her mother.

"Oh, these tomatoes won't do," her mother would say, frowning at the produce. "Your father doesn't like his tomatoes too ripe."

"But I like them ripe," Sara had pointed out.

"I do, too. But I have to put a meal on the table that pleases your father. I like to make him happy. You'll understand someday."

Sara had privately believed she would never understand, and she'd vowed that when she was grown-up she would cook exactly what she liked, husband or no husband. Yet here she was, plotting how to fix food that Reece would like.

And he wasn't anything close to her husband.

What was going on here? Was she secretly more like her mother than she thought?

"You know," she said, "maybe you *should* buy a few foods that you especially like. Then you'll have something to fall back on if you're not wild about my cooking."

"Sara, I never said I don't like your cooking. I think you're amazing in the kitchen."

She knew he was just soothing her ego, and she tried not to feel ridiculously pleased at the compliment.

But she couldn't help the smile that spread across her face. Reece thought she was amazing.

"I WALKED twenty-two steps," Miss Greer said proudly. "Can you believe they have me walking the day after surgery?"

"The doctor said your recovery is going well." Reece was surprised at how chatty Miss Greer was on pain meds. Not out of her head or talking in German, as she'd been yesterday according to Sara, but relaxed and jabbering like a magpie.

"So how's everything back at the castle?" Miss Greer asked. "I understand you fixed breakfast yesterday." She didn't seem distressed by that idea.

"Sara did all the cooking. I just put it on the table."

"She's a good girl, that one. You're not letting her handle the money, are you?"

"No, ma'am. I ran the credit cards for the guests."

"Good. Now, Reece, I want you to do something for me. There's a girl here who's been taking care of me—I want to give her some money, but I don't have any cash with me."

"You want to…what?" Were the hospital staff shaking down Miss Greer?

"She's not a nurse, just a volunteer, and she's been so sweet and I know she could use some extra cash."

"Miss Greer, I don't think that's a good idea." The woman was on heavy drugs and she might not be thinking right. "Did she ask you for money?"

"Oh, heavens, no. Her name is Fatima. I don't have any cash in my purse, but I have some at home. Could you get out…oh, about a hundred dollars and make sure that Fatima gets it?"

Normally Miss Greer was extremely prudent with her money. "Why don't you wait until you're at home, and send it to her?" Reece suggested.

"My secret stash is under my mattress. Just bring the money next time you visit. Or send it with Sara."

Now he knew Miss Greer wasn't in her right mind. No one who knew Sara would give her a hundred dollars to deliver. Not that she would steal it—never that. But what if it got mixed up in her money ball? At the very least, the bills would get all wrinkled. If she didn't give them to some homeless person.

"I'll do that," he said to appease Miss Greer. Chances were by tomorrow she would forget all about it. Later, if she really did want to send a gift to Fatima, she could still do so.

"Well, I expect you've humored me long enough," she said. "*Jeopardy*'s on. I want to watch that."

"Are you sure there's nothing else you need?"

"They're taking good care of me here, don't worry."

They were drugging her up, that was for sure. He'd never seen her so cheerful.

"You and Sara enjoy the evening. Why don't you go to a movie or something?"

Reece coughed to disguise his reaction. "Sara and me?" Why would she say that? Had Sara mentioned their quasi-date?

"Come on now, Reece," Miss Greer said with a smile. "I've seen the way you look at her. Have you tried asking her out on a date? I know she's not dating anyone."

"I'm not really Sara's type," he said diplomatically.

"Her type are all flakes. Artists, musicians, movie directors, starving actors. She could use a boyfriend with a head on his shoulders."

"I'll make a deal with you. I'll let you play matchmaker with me if you return the favor. How about that nice man who owns Old Salt's Bar and Grill? He's a widower, nice-looking—"

Miss Greer tittered like a schoolgirl. "Don't be silly. I'm allowed to play matchmaker—I'm an old woman. Now be gone with you. Alex Trebek is on."

LATER THAT AFTERNOON, Allie came over to the B and B. Cooper was handling the afternoon charter on his own, since it was only a couple of passengers, and Allie had decided she would visit Miss Greer. Sara asked to tag along, solving her transportation problem, and afterward they were going to do some wedding planning.

"So how are you managing without Miss Greer?" Allie asked as soon as Sara was buckled into the passenger seat of Allie's little blue Suzuki Rodeo.

That was a very good question. "Okay, I guess. Reece is helping."

Allie raised her eyebrows. "No kidding? Does he wear a frilly apron and scrub bathtubs?"

Sara let herself form that mental picture, then embellished it slightly, picturing him in the frilly apron—and nothing else. Surprisingly sexy.

"Sara?"

She snapped back to the present. "He makes beds. And he serves breakfast. Unfortunately, he also put Miss Greer's good china in the dishwasher."

"That's bad?"

Of course Allie wouldn't understand. She was a tomboy through and through and had probably never had a dishwasher. Or fine china, for that matter.

"It's bad. Now we have to try to replace it before Miss Greer gets home from the hospital, and it's a rare pattern. Reece found a few saucers on the Internet, but that's it."

"Hmm. Are you talking about those white dishes with the pink roses?"

Sara nodded.

"I saw some of those somewhere. I remember thinking, hey, those are just like the ones at the Sunsetter."

Sara sat up straighter, nearly strangling herself on the shoulder harness. "Oh, think, Allie! Where did you see them? Was it recently?"

"It seems I was with Cooper, so pretty recently. Maybe at one of those antique stores on Second Street."

"Which one?"

Allie shrugged. "They all run together in my mind."

At least it was a place to start. There were probably a dozen antiques stores in Port Clara's old downtown, but it wouldn't take that long to hit them all, blitz style.

When they reached Miss Greer's room at the hospital, Reece was just coming out. He looked yummy today in crisp jeans and a shirt with blue stripes, neatly tucked in. At least he'd gone to short sleeves in deference to the warmer May weather, but the shirt was starched to within an inch of its life.

Allie greeted him with a hug, which was a little bit funny when Sara thought about it. A few short weeks ago, all of the Remingtons had been Allie's enemies, trying to take away her boat and her livelihood. Now she was marrying into their family.

"No cruise today?" Reece asked her.

"Cooper's handling it. I needed an afternoon off and some girl talk."

"How is she?" Sara whispered, nodding toward the partially open door.

"Health-wise, pretty well," Reece replied. "She's been up walking, and she's a regular Chatty Cathy. But I'm afraid I upset her."

Sara gasped. "You didn't tell her about the dishes, did you? Because I have a lead on some replacements."

"No. But I…well, I asked her about the future. She was worried about whether she could keep running the B and B, and I asked her if she'd planned for retirement and if she had long-term care insurance and…and, well, she got upset."

"Of course she did! Nobody wants to think about being shuffled off to the old folks home, especially when they're lying in a hospital bed."

"I'm worried about her. She keeps her money under her mattress, for pity's sake."

"It makes her feel safe," Sara pointed out sensibly. "She went through a war, remember. Maybe her parents were able to escape Germany because they *did* have a cash reserve."

Reece looked thoughtful. "I never thought of that. Would you try to calm her down? I didn't mean to upset her."

Allie slipped into the room, leaving Reece and Sara alone. "I'm sure you meant well, Reece, but not everyone sees the world like you. As cautious as Miss Greer is with her money, I'm sure she has some saved for a rainy day, which is better than a lot of people."

"What if she becomes disabled? What if her mind goes? She has no family to take care of her. Someone could take advantage of her."

"She has lots of friends. I love her like my own grandmother, Reece. I won't let anything bad happen to her." She supposed Reece saw that as the blind taking care of the blind, but she refused to spend her days worrying about the future. Life was too short.

Impulsively she leaned up and kissed his cheek. "You're sweet to worry. But you really need to lighten up. Live in the moment. Smile a little more. Carpe diem."

He took a deep breath and forced a smile. "I'll try."

"I'm going to a party tonight. Why don't you come with me?"

"On a Sunday?"

"What's wrong with having a party on Sunday? It's still the weekend."

"I have some financials I have to go over tonight."

She rolled her eyes. "Suit yourself," she said, as if it made no difference to her. But inside she wilted. She'd asked him out and he'd turned her down. She had to face it—he wasn't into her. Yeah, maybe they had chemistry, but Reece was obviously the kind of man who needed more.

She wasn't convinced that there couldn't *be* more, but apparently he was.

He said goodbye and walked away, and Sara swallowed the stupid lump in her throat and entered Miss Greer's room, nearly hitting Allie, who was on her way out.

"Sorry," she said.

"Sorry," Allie said at the same time. "I was just coming to see what happened to you. Did you just ask Reece to go to a party with you?"

"You were eavesdropping."

"No, honestly, I wasn't. The door was open a crack."

"Well, yes, I asked him, and he said no." Sara brushed past Allie into the room. "Hello, Miss Greer!" she said cheerily. "How are you today?"

"I was fine, until Reece reminded me that I'm going to end up bankrupt in a nursing home, dependent on the kindness of strangers."

Sara sighed. "Don't listen to him," she said, rubbing

the elderly lady's arm. "He means well, really, but his brain functions a bit differently from ours."

"Actually," Allie said, "Reece is very good at what he does. I had a little bit saved for retirement, but not nearly enough. After he ran the numbers for me I realized I had to do more—"

"Wait a minute," Sara interrupted. "You're not taking his side, are you?"

"I don't see it as taking sides," Allie said. "I'm just saying everyone should do some planning for the future. Everyone," she added pointedly, giving Sara a meaningful look.

"And I say that if you spend today worrying about the future, you've wasted a perfectly good day."

"Oh, Reece is probably right," Miss Greer grumbled. "I won't live forever. You won't either, Sara. You're young and healthy now, but in the blink of an eye, you're old and you wonder what happened to the years."

Great. Now she'd lost Miss Greer to the dark side.

"Can we change the subject to something more cheerful? We could talk about my root canal." An aide chose that moment to deliver Miss Greer's lunch, and no more was said about retirement, which suited Sara just fine.

AFTER LEAVING the hospital, Sara and Allie went to Allie's house to talk about the wedding. Allie had no interest in an expensive gown or a tall cake, or forcing her friends to wear ugly bridesmaids' dresses. But she did want to mark the occasion in a special and memorable way. So she and Cooper were renting the biggest party barge they could find and decking it out with flowers stem to stern. They were inviting close friends on an afternoon wedding cruise, complete with champagne and appetizers. Afterward there would be a big party on the beach for everybody who wanted to come. Practically the whole town knew Allie, and they all wanted to raise a glass in honor of her nuptials.

"I love this house," Sara commented as they settled in the den, which was littered with several dresses in bags, shoes, recipes, bridal magazines, florists' catalogs and a stack of half-addressed invitations. "I'm so glad Cooper decided to rent it."

"We're talking about buying it," Allie said. "It's perfect for us."

"And for the bambinos you'll have," Sara added. "You're going to have twelve so their devoted auntie Sara can spoil them rotten, right?"

"First I have to survive the wedding." Allie looked uneasily at the wedding-planning detritus. "I wanted to keep it simple, and now it's getting out of hand. Is it too late to elope?"

"Just start making decisions," Sara said practically. "I'll help you finish addressing the invitations."

"Ah, no, thanks. I've got that covered."

"It's my handwriting, right?" Sara tried not to feel slighted. Her penmanship was abominable.

"That, and the fact you'll transpose numbers and misspell names. But there is something really important you can do. I know you're superbusy with Miss Greer's surgery and all, but I need a caterer. I was going to fix the food myself, but—"

"I'd be honored! You'll be way too busy to worry about that."

"Can you do that and be my maid of honor, too?"

"Of course. I'll fix everything ahead of time. How about a Southwestern theme for the food? Taquitos and flautas, nachos—"

"Whatever you want. For about fifty people. If I can just scratch it off my list and turn it over to you, I'd be so grateful."

"Give me a budget, then say no more. What about cakes?"

"We're doing just one cake, from Rominelli's Bakery. No punch or anything fussy, just champagne and soft drinks."

"I can do all that, too."

With the food and drink portion of the planning taken care of, they moved on to dress and shoe modeling and picking out flowers. For once, Allie allowed herself to be a girlie-girl, choosing pink and white roses and carnations.

Sara had to admit she felt a little wistful. As a girl, she'd never been entranced with the idea of being a bride. She'd preferred fantasizing that she was a secret agent or a rock star. Later, she had decided she would never get married—too restrictive. She hated the thought of being tied down.

But seeing Allie in her slightly stressed state of romantic bliss had given birth to fantasies of Prince Charming and happily ever after.

Where was that damn prince, anyway?

She thought briefly of Reece, then shook her head.

"What's wrong?" Allie asked.

"What? Nothing."

"You looked sad all the sudden."

"Allie, is there something wrong with me?"

"What? No. What could be wrong with you? You're perfect."

Sara snorted at that one. She was far from perfect, but neither did she think she was repulsive. "Reece is attracted to me—I know he is. He's hetero and unattached. So why can't I, you know, get something going with him?"

Allie's eyebrows rose so high they almost joined her hairline. "This is something you want? I mean, I agree that Reece has a little thing for you. I've seen him watching you with this expression of…I don't know. Wonder, I guess."

"Wonder?"

"Like he's watching an exotic, alien creature."

That didn't sound so nice.

"But I didn't think you would be interested in someone so…how do I put this?"

"Boring? A stick-in-the-mud?"

"Now, I wouldn't have put it that way. But he is more conservative than your usual type of boyfriend."

"But maybe I need a different kind of boyfriend. All those guys I've dated—what's it ever gotten me? They're usually flakier than me, even. No stability, no clue about commitment, not exactly loyal…"

"But I thought you wanted someone to have adventures with."

"I do, but I just realized I also want someone I can depend on. Someone who can ground me."

"Okay, but maybe you should make the change

slowly, by degrees. No more Peter Pans, but someone with a pulse."

"Allie! Reece has a pulse." She thought about that hot kiss outside his room. Even the memory made her feel a bit melty. "You should have seen how well he dealt with Miss Greer's accident. He was calm and efficient, but kind, too. And he didn't have to agree to help out at the B and B, but he did. He even tried Bulgarian food."

"Really. You two have been out together?"

"Sort of. But I guess it wasn't as much fun for him as it was for me. Maybe I should have let him take me to a steak house like he wanted."

A mischievous smile spread across Allie's face. "If you want Reece, then I think you should have him. But he seems shy. You're going to have to make the first move."

"I already made the first move. I asked him to come with me to the party and he turned me down, remember?" Sara looked away, refusing to admit how much his turndown bothered her. "How many first moves do I have to make before I admit defeat?"

Chapter Six

Reece spent most of the afternoon going over the dratted financials and painstakingly explaining the concept of Collateralized Mortgage Obligation over the phone to his brother, who was handling the financial aspects of a leveraged buyout.

But his thoughts were never far from Sara.

He'd blown it in more ways than one today. First he'd upset Miss Greer with his talk about nursing homes. Then he'd argued with Sara. And finally, when she'd overlooked his boorish behavior and actually asked him to go to a party with her, he'd said no.

The answer was automatic reflex. The thought of going out for a purely social evening with Sara terrified him. He didn't much like parties, either.

But she'd asked him out. And he'd said no.

Maybe he needed to read a book on interpersonal skills, because he obviously was lacking in them. While he was at it, maybe he should see a shrink, too. He was crazy for being so attracted to Sara, and also crazy for pulling away from her when she'd made an overture.

He heard the front door open and knew without a doubt it was Sara and not one of the guests. She didn't say anything, but the air in the house subtly changed whenever she entered or exited. Not long ago he would have scoffed at the idea that a person had vibrations that could be sensed, but Sara did.

He had the financial printout, a yellow legal pad and several other documents spread out over the dining-room table. He'd hoped to finish his work early enough to free up his evening—if Sara would give him a second chance at that party.

But he still had several hours' worth of analysis to do, and Bret needed it by tomorrow morning.

He didn't like disappointing his brother, especially at this sensitive time, when Remington Industries was about to name a new VP of Finance, a position currently held by their soon-to-retire father.

Reece and Bret had always gotten along well, but sometimes Bret's meteoric ascent in the family business was irksome. Bret was no smarter than Reece, but he knew how to work the system better. Reece had to remind himself that it wasn't Bret's fault that he was charming and glib; he could shovel manure and make you think it was spun gold. He'd been born that way. But he couldn't work the numbers the way Reece could.

Bret had gotten in over his head with this project, and if Reece were spiteful he would let Bret drown in his own incompetence. But that wasn't his way.

"Oh, hi," Sara said reservedly. "How's it going?"

"Slow. Did you calm Miss Greer down?"

"She's fine. In the end she wasn't really mad at you.

It's just that you made her think about things that made her uncomfortable."

"I got that." He put down his pen, took off his glasses and squeezed the bridge of his nose.

Sara pulled out a chair and sat beside him. "Headache?"

"It's nothing. I probably just need new glasses. I'll take something."

She stood and moved behind him. He tensed because he didn't know what she was going to do. But when she placed her fingertips on his forehead right at the hairline and began moving them in slow, firm circles, he quickly surrendered to it.

Somewhere in the back of his mind, an annoying voice reminded him that letting Sara touch him like this wasn't such a good idea. They were alone in the house—all of the guests had checked out today.

But another, less rational part of him told the annoying voice to shut up. This felt too good to stop.

She moved her fingers to another spot, began the slow massage again, and the muscles of his face relaxed.

"This is much better than any medicine you could take." Her voice was soft, low in her throat.

"I thought you were mad at me."

"Nah. I'm always shooting my mouth off when I shouldn't, but I get over things quickly. No use holding on to anger."

"That's a nice philosophy. Speak your mind, then let it go."

"Yeah. Most people don't get that. They get very attached to their grudges."

Did he hold grudges?

She moved on to his temples, then the top of his jaw. She massaged his ears, then behind his ears. She dug her thumbs into the back of his neck.

Reece let out an involuntary moan.

"Did I hurt you?"

"God, no."

She moved her thumbs down his upper spine, finding each little tight spot and working it loose. She moved on to his shoulders. Her hands were firm, and she seemed to know exactly what she was doing.

Could he hire her to come to New York, stand behind his chair at work and do this…oh, maybe once an hour?

She reached around to his chest and unfastened the top button of his shirt. By now he was such a mound of Jell-O that it didn't register for a few seconds that she was taking off his shirt.

"Um, Sara?"

"Massage is much more effective skin to skin."

I'll say.

The annoying voice started up again, but Reece mentally put a clamp on it as Sara yanked out his shirttails and dragged his shirt off his shoulders and down his arms past his elbows, baring a good part of his upper torso.

She massaged his upper back and arms, digging her thumbs under his shoulder blades. "You're just loaded with tension knots. I can work them loose, but it will hurt a little."

"I don't think you can hurt me—ouch."

"Sorry."

It was a bit uncomfortable as she worked the balled-up muscles, but it was a good kind of hurt, if there was such a thing.

"You have good muscles for an accountant."

"Too skinny," he mumbled. All his life he'd had to work to keep meat on his bones. His brother had played football in high school, and the family always made a big deal about attending the games and cheering him on. Reece hadn't had the body type for football and so had opted for soccer, but he couldn't remember his parents coming to any of his games. His father, though he never said it, clearly thought soccer was for sissies.

"You're not skinny," Sara said firmly. "You're lean. There's a difference. Do you work out?"

"A little." Not as much lately, though. He used to run, but he couldn't remember the last time he'd put on his running shoes.

"How's your headache?" she asked.

"It's…it's gone."

She ran her fingers lightly over his back as she finished up the massage, giving him wonderful chills. "Now, see, wasn't that better than taking some stupid pill that would just mess up your stomach anyway?"

"I would never take another pill in my life if you could cure all problems like that."

She laughed as she pulled his shirt back up onto his shoulders. She gave his upper arms an affectionate squeeze, and she might have even pressed her face against the back of his head, but he wasn't sure about that.

"I'm glad to oblige." Then she moved to pick up her purse where she'd dropped it onto the table. "I'm going to put my things away and change clothes. Any thoughts on dinner?"

"Uh." She was walking away? He'd kind of thought the whole massage thing might be the beginning of a seduction, and he'd been willing to go along with it. Or rather, he'd been helpless to stop it.

But apparently a therapeutic massage was all she'd had in mind.

"Well, you think about it," she said breezily, and she headed for the stairs.

Reece buttoned his shirt and tucked it back into his jeans. Dinner. He was hungry, but could he endure another of Sara's concoctions?

By the time she returned downstairs, Reece had shut down his computer and arranged his papers into neat stacks. He could work on this some more after dinner, but he didn't want to risk the headache returning until he'd eaten.

"I could make BLTs," she said.

That sounded pretty safe. "Okay, thanks."

"On yours I'll use white bread, mayonnaise, iceberg lettuce and nothing weird."

"You make me feel very boring, you know."

"I consider you more of a challenge than boring. The first time I saw you, I remember thinking I wanted to ruffle your hair, mess you up a little."

He couldn't tell her what he'd thought when he first saw her. She would probably slap him. "What time does your party start?"

"Oh, later. Nine or ten o'clock. Sure you don't want to come?"

"Actually, yeah, I'd like to."

She flashed him a brilliant smile. "You mean it? Excellent."

After she disappeared into the kitchen, Reece called his brother on his cell.

"Have you figured out what the problem is?" Bret asked, his voice tense with anxiety.

"I have an idea, but I'm not there yet. Bret, I'm sorry, but it won't be done by tomorrow morning."

Long silence. Then, "Really?"

"Yeah, really." It was probably a shock to Bret. Reece always lived and died by his deadlines. But given the choice between a deadline and Sara, Sara won hands down.

"YOU DON'T NEED your car keys," Sara said as Reece came down the stairs, keys in hand. "We're taking the trolley. That way no one has to be the designated driver."

He'd changed out of his button-down shirt into something a little more party-esque—a golf shirt, green cargo pants and running shoes. Not bad.

"I don't mind being the designated driver," Reece said.

"But the trolley is more fun. Come on. It's just a short walk to the stop. If we hurry we can make the nine o'clock."

She locked the door, then paused on the front porch and reached for Reece. She thought she saw a flare of something in his eyes as she pulled out his tucked-in shirt, but she wasn't sure.

"There. Much better." Then she reached up and mussed his hair for good measure.

"Sara!" He finger-combed it back into place.

"Sorry. Sooner or later I was going to do that."

Reece's cell phone rang. Honestly, his phone rang more than any other person's Sara had ever known.

"Reece Remington. Oh, hi, Bret." He listened patiently as Sara checked his watch, then indicated with sign language that they should hurry. "Let me call you back about that tomorrow, okay?"

After he completed the call, Sara smiled at him. "Why don't you turn that thing off?"

"Turn it off?" He sounded shocked, as if she'd asked him to tear up his tax return.

"Just for one evening. Can't the world turn without you for a few hours?"

He smiled back at her sheepishly. "Sure, why not." He switched off the phone and stuck it in his pocket.

They walked along at a good clip down Magnolia Street toward the ocean. The old-fashioned trolley ran along Second Street, parallel to the beach but one block inland.

"The trolley is already there," Sara said. "We better hurry or it'll leave without us." She grabbed Reece's hand and they ran down the sidewalk. "Wait!" Sara called as the trolley started to move. Benji, the conductor, usually waited for stragglers, but he must not have seen them. "Hurry, Reece, we can still make it."

"What? No, we can't."

Ignoring him, she ran faster, dragging Reece with her.

A group of people already riding on the car urged them on. Reece, with his long legs, ran ahead and jumped on. The trolley was picking up speed and Sara damn near didn't make it. But Reece grabbed her arm and hauled her on board. They collapsed, laughing and gasping for breath, on the first seat they saw while the other passengers cheered their effort.

"You are crazy!" Reece said, still laughing.

Her heart skipped a few beats. Reece was handsome no matter what expression he wore, but seeing him laugh took her breath away.

"You should laugh more," she said.

"If I spent more time around you, I'm sure I would."

"Am I that funny?"

"You're crazy-funny." He ran one finger down her bare arm and she shivered with anticipation, hoping he might kiss her again or at least take her hand or put an arm around her shoulders. But he pulled away and gazed out the window.

Sara felt like she had in junior high with her first crush. With most guys she knew exactly what signals to send and how to interpret the ones she got back. But with Reece, she was never sure. He kept his cards close to the vest.

The trolley lumbered down the center of Second Street through the renovated downtown filled with ice-cream parlors and T-shirt shops, antique stores, a movie theater where they screened old movies for two bucks—which included free popcorn—restaurants, a couple of funky little hotels and more bed-and-breakfasts.

Palm trees towered over the brick streets and restored nineteenth-century buildings. Sara viewed it with new eyes, taking a sudden pride in her adopted hometown.

"It's a nice town," Reece said, as if reading her mind. "I haven't spent much time checking it out."

"It wasn't always this nice. When I first moved here eleven years ago, downtown was run-down and kind of creepy. But once plans were in place to get the trolley going, the place got a face-lift. Port Clara is starting to be a real vacation destination again, like it was a hundred years ago." That was both good and bad. Good for anybody in the tourist industry, like Allie and Miss Greer. But sometimes Sara missed the sleepy backwardness of the old Port Clara.

"Why did you move here?" Reece wanted to know.

"I was really just passing through. I had it in my mind I would go out to California and make my fortune, maybe become a movie star or something. But I saw that Help Wanted sign in Miss Greer's front window, so I stopped on a whim, and that was it."

She realized her whole life was pretty much lived on a whim. That was how she liked it, but it probably gave Reece hives.

She punched him lightly on the arm. "You probably had your whole life mapped out by the time you were twelve."

He grinned. "You really do know me better than I thought."

They rode the trolley all the way to the end of the line. They stepped off the old wooden car. Sara waved to Benji, who began the process of reversing the car for the trip back.

"Where is this party, anyway?" Reece asked.

"It's on that undeveloped stretch of beach toward the

north end of the island, past the jetty. There's no road—
we'll have to walk along the beach."

"Whose party is it?"

"Um…I don't know. But I heard about it from my
friend Tracy, who heard about it from her boyfriend's
brother. I think it's some friend of his."

Reece skidded to a stop. "So we're crashing?"

She smiled indulgently at him. "This isn't the kind of
party where they send out engraved invitations. Someone
just decides to have it, and word gets around. There will
be a keg and maybe some hot dogs, but people bring their
own food and drink if they feel like it."

"Should we bring something?" Reece asked, nodding toward the convenience store that squatted where
Second Street dead-ended.

"Got it covered." She patted her straw bag.

It was only a block to the beach. They crossed the
dunes using a rickety boardwalk, then Sara paused to
take off her sandals, leaning one hand against his shoulder.

"Don't you want to take off your shoes?" she asked.
"No sense walking on the beach with shoes on."

"I guess. Aren't you worried you'll step on something? It's kind of dark."

"This beach is very clean," she said, unconcerned.
"Oh, look how pretty it is with the moon shining on the
water." She ran toward the ocean, holding her arms wide
as if she could hold the whole thing in her embrace.

When she realized a wave was barreling toward her,
she did an abrupt U-turn and ran the other way, holding
her skirt up so it wouldn't get wet.

Reece was just standing there, watching her.

She squealed in delight as the cold water hit her lower legs. "Hey, come on!" She ran back to him and took his hand, urging him to join her in playing tag with the waves.

"I don't want my pants to get wet."

She sighed, then stooped down to untie his shoe-laces and roll up the legs of his cargo pants to just below his knees. "There. Now catch me!" She took off and, moments later, she heard footsteps slapping in the wet sand behind her. She quickly changed direction, ducking when Reece reached out for her and heading toward the waves, where she was sure Reece wouldn't follow.

But she'd underestimated him. He pursued with single-minded determination and caught her right at the water's edge, pulling her close until they were chest to chest.

"Tag." He closed in for what she was sure would be one helluva kiss—they'd been leading up to it all night. She felt his warm breath, then the subtle intake, and…

A wave chose that moment to hit them full force.

Chapter Seven

Sara shrieked in shock at the cold onslaught, then ran to drier ground, laughing. Reece was more sputtering than laughing. He didn't much appreciate having their moment interrupted in such a rude fashion.

"You're all wet!" Sara said through her giggles.

He gave her a hard look. "You are worse than any ten-year-old." But then he couldn't help grinning. She was so beautiful, standing there dripping water. Some of the seawater had splashed upward on impact, dampening her blouse so that it was transparent in places.

He thought about taking up where they'd left off. He was pretty sure she would be amenable. Or she might make him chase her again.

She leaned over to wring out her skirt, and he did the same with the hem of his shirt. Everything from his hips down was soaking, but the evening was warm and his pants were lightweight cotton, so they would dry quickly. He checked his cell phone to see if it had been damaged, but it had stayed dry in his pocket.

Reece located the shoes he'd kicked off just before

chasing Sara, and Sara found her straw bag where she'd dropped it in the sand, but her shoes were missing.

"Those were my favorite sandals," she lamented.

Reece tugged on his own shoes. "We'll find them."

But after a few more minutes, they had to admit defeat.

"They were Mexican huaraches," she said glumly. "I bought them in Taxco for three dollars. They were just getting good and broken in."

He was tempted to offer to take her to Mexico to buy new ones—that was the effect she had on him. But she quickly shook off the misfortune, her ready smile returning.

"Let's go party," she said, taking his hand.

They had to clamber over the big rocks used to build the jetty. Reece climbed ahead of her and offered her a hand to balance, which she accepted, though he suspected she could climb the jetty perfectly well without his aid.

On the other side of the jetty, the beach was littered with broken shells. Sara paused, her teeth tugging at her full lower lip.

"Come on, I'll give you a piggyback ride."

"Okay."

He squatted halfway down, and she climbed up, looping her legs around his waist and her arms around his neck. It was the perfect solution. He got to feel Sara's body pressed against his, her warm breath tickling his ear. And she got to save her feet.

Once they reached the smooth sand, Reece didn't put her down. He continued to carry her along the beach— she was as light as a kitten—and she let him. He could carry her like this all night. Well, if she didn't offer an even more attractive position.

That thought startled him. He'd already made the decision that it was wiser if he and Sara did not become any more entangled. But unless she was some kind of major tease, she would welcome his advances. Every move she'd made tonight seemed part of a giant seduction.

They'd left behind the houses and shacks that lined the beach closer to town.

"Why has no one built up this area?" Reece asked.

"This section of coastline is part of a shorebird sanctuary, so no one can develop it. Technically no one's supposed to build a fire here, either, but the local police never check. So long as we put out the fire when we're done and leave the beach clean, the cops look the other way."

They soon saw the glow of the fire ahead of them. Strains of rock music reached them next. When they drew closer, Reece saw thirty or so people gathered around the fire, sitting on logs or beach chairs or right on the sand. A half-dozen boats of every size and description, from dinghies to yachts, anchored just off-shore, and more boats were arriving. He guessed that was how most people arrived, because they hadn't seen anyone else walking the beach.

"Sara, you made it!"

Reece set Sara down, and she ran up to throw herself into a hug with a shirtless man who bore a surfer's bleached hair and perpetual tan.

Reece felt a twinge of jealousy. He wanted to claim

Sara, throw her over his shoulder caveman style and put every man here on notice that she was his, hands off.

But Sara would never belong to him or any man. Trying to tie her down would be as futile as trying to keep a wave on the sand.

"Good to see you, Josh," she said, releasing him.

A curvy little blonde bounced up wearing shorts and a bikini top. "Hey, Sara." They hugged, too.

Sara dragged Reece forward. "This is Reece. He's…visiting from New York," she said carefully. "Reece, this is David and Tracy. Tracy is my yoga instructor, and David…what are you doing lately, David?"

"As little as possible," he said. Then he shook hands with Reece. "Nice to meet ya."

"Did you all go swimming with your clothes on?" Tracy asked.

"By accident," Sara said with a laugh. She opened her big straw bag and, to Reece's amazement, pulled out a bottle of wine. "Who do I give this to?"

"I'll take it," David said with a grin. "My brother is the one who popped for the keg and the brats."

Sara held the bottle away from him. "If I give this to you, your brother will never see it. Point him out."

"The guy in the red shirt."

Sara moved through the group with the skill of a public-relations executive working an event. She greeted people she knew with hugs and kisses, introduced herself and Reece to people she didn't even know. She delivered the wine to the host, grabbed a handful of potato chips, then headed for the keg.

"I'll get it," Reece said, belatedly jumping forward to do the honors. All the people, the frenzied talking and laughing and the music, had momentarily distracted him from doing his gentlemanly duty. He was terrible at parties, particularly parties at which he didn't know anyone.

He filled a plastic cup with frothy beer for Sara, and one for himself. He wasn't a big drinker, but he enjoyed an occasional beer, and this setting seemed the place for it. Lots of these partygoers were clearly well on their way to inebriation.

Someone was cooking brats over the fire; they smelled wonderful and Reece wished he hadn't already eaten.

Reece was about to suggest they find themselves a place to sit when he spied his cousin Max, dancing with a redhead who had her back to Reece. He shouldn't have been surprised to see Max here. If there was a party to be found, Max found it. He was a purely social animal—hated spending the evening home alone. Back in New York he had lived in a noisy apartment building full of other singles who were always hanging out by the rooftop pool. If he wasn't attending the opening of a new club or entertaining clients at a hot restaurant, he hung with his neighbors or invited people over to watch a sporting event.

"Oh, there's Tandy," Sara said. "She has her baby with her!" And Sara was off, like a honeybee lured by the scent of a new flower.

Reece didn't want to follow her around like a puppy. He headed for Max, whose redheaded partner turned out to be Allie, who was soon to become a part of the Remington family by marrying Cooper.

"Did you steal Cooper's girl already?" he asked when he reached the dancing couple.

"Reece! I didn't expect to see you here." Allie stopped dancing long enough to give Reece a kiss on the cheek.

No, a party was usually the last place anyone expected to find Reece, the family stick-in-the-mud. "I came with Sara." Just in case Max had any ideas about poaching.

Max looked a bit perplexed by that declaration, but Allie grinned widely. "Too cool. Wanna dance? Cooper's all tied up with boat talk." She nodded toward the ocean, where a group of men, including Cooper, were eyeing a beautiful cruiser that seemed to be made of more glass than anything.

"Sure, I'll dance." Dancing wasn't his thing, either, but he took a fortifying gulp of beer and made himself do it. Tonight he was Party Man.

Allie shooed Max away. "Go ask her," she said in a loud stage whisper. "I know you're dying to."

Reece set down his beer, anchoring the cup in the sand and hoping it didn't get kicked over, then took both of Allie's hands in a proper, sisterly dance. Someone had put an oldies CD in the boom box, so they hammed it up, pretending to do the jitterbug when neither of them had a clue how.

He watched Max from the corner of his eye, though. His cousin approached a raven-haired beauty who sat alone in a lawn chair, a darling, blond-headed toddler playing in the sand at her feet.

Max pasted on his patented, never-fail charming

smile and looked as if he was going to work his magic on her. But at the last minute, the smile fled and he changed direction, heading for the keg instead.

"Who's that woman?" Reece asked, nodding toward the quiet brunette.

"Jane. She lives on the boat next door to ours."

"The one with the violent husband?" he asked with some alarm. The day he and his cousins had arrived in Port Clara, Max had made the mistake of flirting with someone named Jane whose husband had taken exception and punched him in the face.

"Not to worry. The husband is soon to be an ex. The divorce is almost final."

"And are you trying to play matchmaker? 'Cause Max always steers clear of single moms."

"Really? Why is that? He doesn't like kids?"

"It's more that he's uncomfortable around them. He dated a woman once who had a little boy, and every time they went out, they had a three-foot chaperone. Left a bad taste in his mouth."

"Ah. Well, that's a shame. They look nice together."

Jane's eyes followed Max to the beer, and Reece suspected some mutual chemistry at work. "Best not to encourage it," he said. "Max is a great guy, but he plays the field. If Jane is smarting from a divorce, she doesn't need games."

"She's not about to get serious, either," Allie said. "If she and Max could have a little fun without everything getting heavy, I think it would be a good thing."

Reece didn't argue further, because he made it a policy never to dabble in other people's relationships.

"Hey, you stole my date!" Sara was right at his elbow, grinning.

"You can have him back. He's wearing me out. Thanks for the dance, Reece." Allie stood on her tiptoes and kissed him on the cheek again, then drifted off.

Sara leaned on Reece's shoulder. "How 'bout it, sailor? Wanna dance?"

Not really. What had seemed a harmless, low-pressure activity with Allie was altogether different with Sara. He couldn't hold both her hands as he'd done with Allie—that was far too brotherly. But if he took her in his arms like he wanted to, he would be expected to actually dance.

Sara solved the problem by hooking her arms around his neck and placing her bare feet on top of his shoes.

Deciding to go with the flow, he slid his arms around Sara, holding her close, and moved to the music, which was thankfully a slower song, an Elvis ballad.

She looked up at him, eyes bright. "Are you having fun?"

"I am now."

"I love parties. Don't you?"

"Not so much."

"Really?" She seemed shocked that anyone wouldn't enjoy something she clearly thrived on. "How come?"

He could have told her he was a classic introvert, that he preferred the company of a few close friends—or even solitude—to a big crowd, or that being surrounded by loud noise and confusion frazzled his nerves.

Instead he said, "Because I don't want to share you."

That made her smile. "Well, okay then."

She laid her head on his shoulder and let her fingers play with the hair at the nape of his neck.

Time stood still as he held her so close they moved as one, inhaling the vanilla scent of her hair, feeling her breasts rise and fall as she softly breathed.

But the song ended and someone had the gall to follow the ballad with hip-hop, something with a rowdy beat and nasty lyrics.

Sara stepped off his feet and looked up at him. "Thank you, that was lovely."

Reece thought quickly. How could he hold on to the mood? *Get her alone.* Well, duh. It was hard to maintain intimacy in a big crowd where the music was so loud they could barely talk. Whatever birds were being "protected" here had probably flown their nests and headed for South America.

He grabbed her hand. "Come with me."

She nodded, picked up her purse and her drink, and followed without hesitation, which said something about her level of trust. Or maybe it just said she thought he was harmless.

Hand in hand, they walked up the beach, still heading north, until the party sounds became muffled.

"Sorry if I'm taking you away from all the fun," he said, pausing to look out over the water. A ship, all lit up, was heading north, also, probably toward Galveston or Houston.

"As far as I'm concerned, the fun's here. I take it with me wherever I go. Hey, that's a cruise ship. Have you ever been on a cruise?"

"Me? God, no. I get seasick, remember?"

"I've never been on a cruise, either, but I've applied for jobs with all the major cruise lines. I could see more of the world that way."

The thought of her hopping a cruise ship troubled him. She would be completely inaccessible then. It was the one place he couldn't follow her.

Follow her? Where had that come from? He had a life back home. It was all planned out. He had a damn fine salary, a home, his family, a history. Was he thinking he would chuck it all and go knocking about the world with Sara, living on love? That sort of fantasy was for fools.

"Have you done much traveling?" Sara asked.

"Not much. I went on vacations with my parents when I was a kid—mostly to golf resorts." His dad—and later, Bret—would play golf all day; his mother would spend hours at the spa; Reece would be entertained by a babysitter. When he went to Hawaii, he saw nothing but the inside of the hotel and the swimming pool.

"I've never stayed at a resort. Is it nice?"

He shrugged. "It's okay. The best part was ordering room service. I could get exactly what I wanted."

"Hamburgers and French fries for every meal?"

He laughed. "Pretty much."

Once the cruise ship slipped from view they started walking again. The beach petered out, turning from sand to rocks, so they headed inland toward the dunes.

"Let's look for shooting stars," she said.

Reece eyed the nearest sand dune dubiously. His clothes were still damp, and if he sat in the sand he would be coated in the gritty stuff.

But Sara had that covered. She reached into her purse and pulled out a small ball of wadded-up fabric. To his amazement, when she shook it out it was the size of a blanket.

"So we don't get sand all over us."

He helped her spread the fabric at the edge of the dune. It was as thin as tissue paper. "What is this?"

"It's from India—isn't it wonderful? Batik silk. I never go anywhere without it because it comes in so handy."

"You've been to India?" he asked as they settled onto the cloth. He leaned back against the dune and looked up at the stars.

"Once. It's an amazing place, both beautiful and harsh. Tracy and I have talked about going back. She wants to do an intensive yoga study there." She sighed. "But there's not enough money right now."

Reece had never had even a fleeting desire to visit India—or even an Indian restaurant. But hearing the wistfulness in her voice, he wished he could take her there.

That was the kind of guy Sara needed—someone who would take off for India on a whim.

They both lay back against the dune, gazing up at the crystal clear sky. No wonder Remington Charters' stargazer cruises were so popular. The stars here were amazing.

But the woman next to him was even more so. As her eyes scanned the heavens for her much-hoped-for shooting star, Reece's eyes scanned her. She was so beautiful, it made his heart ache and other parts of him misbehave.

He wanted to kiss her again. But a woman like Sara—so open with her affections—probably had trouble with guys pushing themselves on her, when maybe all she wanted was to share a nice view of the ocean. If he weren't a decent guy, she could be in big trouble right now.

"There's one!" she cried excitedly, pointing toward the sky. "Did you see it?"

"I was looking at you," he admitted.

She turned to him, her mouth parted slightly in her excitement. "You have to watch, or you can't make a wish."

"Did you make a wish?" he asked.

"Well, I started to wish for a trip to India," she said. "But then I realized there's something else I want more."

"What's that?"

Her eyes burned with sudden intensity. "You."

Reece's mouth went dry, and he realized *he* was the one in trouble.

Chapter Eight

Sara held her breath. Had she really just said that? Oh, she just couldn't help herself. From the moment they'd run to catch the trolley and had landed on the seat together, laughing and out of breath, to chasing each other and the almost kiss just before getting soaked, holding hands, dancing, talking…

Everything he said, everything he did, made her want him more.

She knew she was being forward, which was what Allie had suggested. She claimed that Reece was enough of a gentleman that he wouldn't come on to her unless he was sure she absolutely welcomed his attentions.

Well, he shouldn't harbor any doubts now. She'd made herself pretty clear.

Reece stared at her for several heartbeats, and then suddenly she found herself flat on her back. Reece had her shoulders pressed into the ground with his hands, and he loomed over her like some kind of ocean god.

"You drive me absolutely wild, woman, I hope you know that."

"That's kind of the idea, right?"

In answer he kissed her. Not the slow, teasing, sensual kiss he'd treated her to the other night, but a high-energy hurricane of a kiss. His mouth was hard on hers as he held her a willing prisoner against their make-shift bed.

Her body came alive, instantly hot and ready, clamoring for his touch. She had never wanted any man the way she wanted Reece Remington.

She could smell the salt on his skin, mixed with the heady scent of sandalwood soap—the soap she herself placed in his shower whenever she cleaned his room.

Sara ran her hands under his shirt along the smooth skin of his back. He groaned deep in his throat every time she moved, no matter where she touched.

But he wasn't touching her in the same way. Other than his feverish kiss, and hands on her shoulders, he hadn't touched her. She took his right hand and boldly guided it onto her breast.

That was all the encouragement he needed. Then his hands were all over her, touching her everywhere, through her clothes, under her clothes. He pushed her blouse above her breasts, puzzled briefly over the front clasp of her bra, then unfastened it. He pressed his face against her bare breasts, rubbing the hard nipples against his jaw, letting his slight beard stubble abrade them.

She nearly came out of her skin. No man had ever done that before. But Reece, overcome with passion though he was, was still attuned to her feelings. That knowledge gave her a warm glow deep inside her chest that had nothing to do with the actual lovemaking.

Her clothing began to feel like a straitjacket, and she pushed Reece away long enough that she could drag the blouse over her head and shimmy out of the skirt.

"Oh, Sara." His voice was rough with emotion, and to her surprise her eyes welled up slightly with feelings she couldn't even name. What had started as something of a game with Reece, seeing if she could get him to lose control, had become much, much more.

She wasn't simply a conquest to Reece. This wasn't just two people coming together as consenting adults and enjoying each other's bodies. This was making love in the fullest sense of the term.

Reece yanked off his shirt; the rest of his clothes soon followed and they were skin to glorious skin, wrapped around each other until Sara couldn't tell where she ended and he began. His arousal pressed against her belly, and she thought she was going to pass out if he didn't do something with it soon. She spread her legs and wrapped them around his hips in silent invitation, just in case he had missed the fact she was ready—more than ready. She was insanely ready.

He sheathed himself inside her in one stroke, and for several moments they both were exquisitely still, enjoying every nuance of this new, more intimate joining. Her body stretched to accommodate all of him, and he pushed in even deeper, to the very heart of her.

This was all she needed. When he renewed his kisses she felt the first tingles of what she knew would be a massive climax, one that in all honesty had started hours ago.

He began to move then, slowly at first, and the tingles

in her body built in intensity, growing into ripples and then waves and waves of pleasure as his rhythm increased and his thrusting became more frenzied.

She sobbed, completely overwhelmed as she crested. Reece's body convulsed with one final, deep thrust, and then he slumped against her, whispering her name over and over into her ear.

He rolled slightly to the side so he wasn't pressing his entire weight into her, but not enough to pull their bodies apart. She didn't want him to withdraw. She wanted to stay like this indefinitely as the waves of pleasure diminished, leaving in their wake a warm glow.

She shivered, and Reece pulled the edges of the silk cloth around them like a cocoon. She snuggled against him, shifting to a more comfortable position.

They could have stayed there all night if they wanted, she realized. The bed-and-breakfast was empty of guests. No one would notice if they didn't come home.

But she had a feeling Reece wasn't a sleep-on-the-beach kind of guy. For that matter, he probably wasn't normally a sex-on-the-beach kind of guy either. She wondered how he would deal with his loss of control.

A few minutes later she had her answer.

"Sara?"

"Yes, Reece?"

"We didn't use any kind of protection."

Sara sighed and propped her head up on her elbow so she could see his face. His expression gave her serious pause. He looked pretty grim.

She ran a finger along his jaw. "Oh, you silver-tongued devil. I think that's the most romantic thing any man has ever said to me right after sex." Okay, she would have preferred, *You're the best I've ever had, you're incredible, you're the most beautiful, sexiest creature in the universe....* But thinking about protecting her was certainly better than *I have to go,* or, *Is there any pizza left?*

"I've never done that." His voice was filled with what Sara could only describe as despair. "I've never just…forgotten before."

No, she didn't imagine he had. He probably scheduled his sex, wrote it down in his Day-Timer.

"Please don't worry," she said, knowing she had to allay his fears. "I'm on the pill."

"Oh. Oh, that's good." His relief was palpable.

"You don't have to worry about catching anything, either. I've been celibate for a while, and my last checkup was good."

"You're not worried about catching something from me?"

"Not at all. Because I'm willing to bet you have a battery of tests done every six months, just to be on the safe side. Whether you've had sex or not."

"You know, it's getting a little scary, the way you've figured me out. Am I all that predictable?"

She laughed. "No. I never would have predicted this."

"You make me act like a crazy person."

She played with the dusting of hair on his chest. "It's fun being crazy."

"It makes me nervous." He ignored her playful caresses and sat up, rubbing his face. "I hold an executive position at a multinational corporation, responsible for decisions that could bring the company millions of dollars—or lose it. I don't have sex on public beaches." He moved away from her and started hunting for his clothes.

Sara heaved a big sigh and sat up, also. She knew this had been too good to last. While his hormones were running amok, his conservative, sound judgment went right out the window, which was fine with her. But now it was back.

She pulled on her clothes, wondering how to recapture the intimacy they'd so recently shared.

When they were both dressed, Sara shook out their impromptu beach blanket and loosely folded it into a long strip, which she wrapped around her shoulders like a shawl. It had grown cooler, and not just between her and Reece.

"We should head back to the Sunsetter," he said. "It's getting late."

She saluted him. "Sir, yes, sir."

That stopped him. "I'm being a complete ass, aren't I?"

"Absolutely."

He pulled her to him and wrapped his arms around her. "God, I'm sorry, Sara. This has been an incredible night, all the way around, starting with the sandwiches—all of it. You're the most...I don't even know how to describe you. Beautiful, passionate, generous—that's not enough."

"Okay, you're forgiven for being an ass."

"You deserve champagne and a feather bed strewn with rose petals, not flat beer and a roll in the sand."

She extracted herself from his embrace so she could

look at him. "You're kidding, right? We made love under the stars. No girl could ask for better. And if you would stop overanalyzing everything for one second and enjoy the moment, you would see I'm right."

"But…"

"But *what?* You're venturing into ass territory again. You think this was just a roll in the sand, huh? Is that all it meant to you?"

His eyes widened. "No, no."

"All right, then. Look, if you're worried that now I have big expectations, that I'll be hinting around for an engagement ring or wanting to take you home to meet my parents, don't worry. I'm the girl who doesn't plan for the future, remember? I know you're returning to New York. I know I can't go with you. I'm okay with that. But that doesn't mean tonight is trivial, not to me, anyway."

"Not to me, either, Sara. I didn't mean to give you that impression. Don't be angry with me, okay? I'm not very good at living in the moment, so I'm bound to make mistakes."

"Are we going to spend the night together?" she asked.

"Is that what you want?"

"I asked first."

"I would like very much to go to sleep with you in my arms. In a nice, soft bed."

She slid her arm around his waist and hooked her thumb in one of his belt loops. "Then I'm not angry."

THERE HADN'T BEEN MUCH sleeping going on.

By the time they had arrived back at the Sunsetter, Reece had been looking at her as if she were a tasty morsel, the best oyster in the dozen, and for once he hadn't guarded his feelings.

His intense scrutiny had made her squirm, and they hadn't even made it all the way upstairs before clothes went flying again.

Reece was one of the most passionate, creative lovers Sara had ever known. Not that she'd had legions of lovers, but she'd had enough hamburger to know prime rib when she saw it.

She'd lost track of how many times they made love during the night. But she'd fallen into a deep, satisfied sleep in Reece's four-poster bed some time before dawn, not caring how late she slept in because she wasn't needed for breakfast.

When she awoke, the sun was high in the sky, streaming through the lace curtains, and she was alone in the bed.

Darn it.

There was a note on Reece's pillow. She snatched it up and read it greedily. It informed her he had an early meeting at the bank and he hadn't wanted to wake her.

That was sweet.

At least it gave her some time alone to think.

As she showered, feeling deliciously sore in all the right places, she wondered whether spending the night with Reece was an isolated incident, or if they would spend every free moment having wild sex until his return to New York.

And would he go public? Would they be a couple, even temporarily?

Last night she'd bravely told him she was okay

knowing they had no future. But it wasn't entirely true. When it came to Reece, she wasn't quite the free spirit she wanted everyone to believe she was.

She couldn't help envisioning a future with him, tentatively picturing various ways they could stay together. Maybe it had something to do with hormones, or maybe some part of her couldn't link "Reece" and "casual sex" in the same sentence. Somewhere along the way, he had started to matter. A lot.

She called the hospital and talked to Miss Greer, who sounded good and said the doctor might let her go home as soon as tomorrow.

"That's wonderful!" Sara said, trying to inject some enthusiasm into her voice. Of course she wanted her employer to make a swift and painless recovery. But once Miss Greer was back home, things wouldn't be the same with her and Reece. Their partnership would be over, as Miss Greer could resume running the business.

The house had to be sparkling when Miss Greer returned, so Sara threw herself into housework, trying not to worry. That was Reece's job. She had to change all the linens—she'd gotten lazy yesterday. Then she attacked the mountain of laundry, vacuumed and dusted.

It was two o'clock when she realized she hadn't eaten all day, so she went to the kitchen and heated up some leftover frittata and a couple of flour tortillas.

Still Reece hadn't returned. Was he avoiding her?

Finally she heard the front door open as she was putting dishes in the dishwasher. She resisted the urge to run to the door and throw her arms around him. She would have to let him set the pace.

She heard footsteps going up the stairs, then above her head. But only moments later they came down again, and Reece appeared in the kitchen. Looking for her?

"Hey."

"Hi, there," she said cheerfully. "How did your meeting go?"

"It was fine."

She glanced up at the clock on the wall. "It was long."

"I was taking care of some other things. Do you mind if I make myself a sandwich?"

"Make yourself at home. But I can fix something for you."

"A sandwich I can manage." He draped his suit jacket over the back of a chair and opened the refrigerator.

Probably safer, she reasoned. If he built his own sandwich, he could be sure nothing exotic or spicy wound up between the bread slices.

She invented kitchen busywork for herself, studying him covertly while he went about the business of getting out the bread, ham, cheese and mayonnaise. He looked better in a suit than any man she'd ever known. Then again, she hadn't known any but him who wore suits.

"Have any calls come in?"

"A few inquiries regarding our room rates. One reservation."

"Sorry I wasn't here to do my part."

"That's okay. I talked to Miss Greer. She'll be coming home in a day or two."

"That's good. Do you want to visit her today?"

"Are you willing to drive me?" No way was she borrowing his car again. Not that he would let her.

"Sure." Just then Reece's phone rang. "Reece Remington," he answered, as if he were at the office. "Oh, hi, Dad." He sounded wary and looked annoyed.

The dryer buzzer sounded from the laundry room, and Sara used it as her excuse to escape. She wasn't sure why she wanted to, except Reece wasn't acting like the solicitous, smitten lover she'd hoped for. In fact, he was acting the same as he always did.

Did that mean it was over? Had he cured his temporary insanity?

She haphazardly folded sheets while she lectured herself not to overreact. One day at a time, one hour at a time. Yes, in weak moments she let herself believe that Reece might be different from the rest, that they could somehow carve a relationship that would last. Like, forever. But she knew her hopes were unreasonably high.

She carried a stack of messily folded sheets—Miss Greer, queen of the hospital corners, would have a fit—upstairs to the linen closet. Hers was the only bed she hadn't made up today, so she grabbed a set of sheets and headed up to the third floor.

A white shopping bag was propped against her bedroom door.

Her heart pounded, because she knew it hadn't been there earlier. Therefore, it came from Reece. She dropped the sheets and reached for it, peeking inside, where she spied…a pair of shoes?

She pulled them out of the bag. They were Mexican huaraches, almost identical to the ones she'd lost last night. She slipped one onto her bare foot. It fit perfectly.

Flowers would have been nice. Dreamily romantic. But shoes? The best present from a man, ever. It meant he was paying attention to her. He'd seen that she was sad over losing her favorite shoes, and he had made the effort to give her a gift he knew would make her happy. He'd even gotten her size right.

She ran down the stairs, wearing one shoe and carrying the other, not stopping until she reached the kitchen, where Reece sat in the breakfast nook with his sandwich halfway to his mouth.

She launched herself at him and threw her arms around him, not caring if it was the wrong thing to do or whether she got mayonnaise everywhere. She nearly knocked his chair over.

"You are the best! What a thoughtful gift."

He looked a little embarrassed. "Are they the right size? I had to guess."

"They're perfect. Where on earth did you find them?"

"At the drugstore, believe it or not. I went in to buy shaving cream, and there they were."

So he hadn't spent all day scouring import shops and shoe stores, looking for just the right shoe. Didn't matter. It was still thoughtful. She kissed him on the cheek, then reluctantly let him go.

"Those saucers you ordered arrived today," she said.

He shook his head grimly. "We're going to have to tell her, you know. There's no way we can replace everything by the time she comes home."

"Oh, that reminds me—Allie gave me a lead. She said she saw those exact dishes at one of the antique shops downtown."

"Really? Which one?"

"That's the problem. She doesn't remember. But I was thinking of heading out there this afternoon. I could hit most of the stores in a couple of hours, before they close."

A grin lit his face. "I'll go with you. Then we can go to the hospital."

"Sounds good! I'll get my purse." She shoved the other shoe onto her foot, then ran upstairs to grab her purse and put on lipstick.

She realized, as she spritzed on perfume, that she was acting as if this was a date, and she was as excited as if Reece had invited her to a symphony and dinner at the Ritz-Carlton.

"Whoa, girl," she said as she used a tissue to wipe off the perfume. "Don't try so hard." If she wasn't careful, she would scare him so bad she would ruin whatever time they had left.

Chapter Nine

"Oh, look at these hats!" Sara grabbed the biggest, gaudiest one of the display, a blue velvet number with an enormous ostrich plume, and plopped it on her head, then searched for a mirror so she could see herself. She swiveled and found one right behind her. "What do you think? Is it me?"

Reece couldn't help but laugh. She looked like a nineteenth-century strumpet. "Very fetching, Eliza Doolittle, but we have work to do." He snatched the hat off her head and placed it back on the mannequin's head. "Let's find the dishes."

"I just love antique stores. I never buy anything because, well, I don't have anywhere to put stuff, and the Sunsetter has all the antiques it needs. But I love to look. Oh, I see some dishes."

They were white. They had pink roses. But they weren't the right pattern.

Unfortunately, the first store they'd entered was not well organized. Victorian picture frames were displayed right next to a 1930s radio; vintage Mexican pottery sat on a French walnut table. Dishes were strewn all over the store.

"I see some china over there."

Sara didn't answer, so Reece turned around and found she had darted off to another part of the store, where she examined some rather ordinary-looking sheets.

He joined her. "What are you doing?"

"These are hundred-percent cotton sheets and they're a steal," she whispered. "I have to get them."

"We need to focus."

She sighed. "All right. But aimless roaming is much more fun."

They asked the store's owner if she had any of the prized dishes, but the woman had no idea. So they hunted. Twenty minutes later, they had finished with their first store and left empty-handed.

"Let's try that one over there," Sara said, darting across the street and nearly getting run over by a bicycle. She seemed unfazed by the near-collision and headed resolutely toward the store she'd spotted. Reece saw a perfectly good antiques store right next door to the one they'd just exited, and it seemed reasonable to check it first. But Sara was already gone.

They probably should split up. They could cover more territory. But then he would miss watching Sara's delight as she discovered some useless froufrou—a single eggcup shaped like a chicken, for example. Her uninhibited joy reminded him of a kitten that sees every object in the room as a toy to pounce on.

What must it be like, he wondered, to see the world as an endless array of delightful possibilities? He couldn't even imagine it. He'd never been like that, not even as a child. In fact, as a little kid on Christmas morning he would open one present, thoroughly study it, read the instructions if there were any, and play with it until someone reminded him he had more gifts to unwrap.

"I have to look at the books," she said in their third store, distracted once again. "Look at this one! It's an illustrated *Huckleberry Finn* from the 1930s. I know someone who would love to add this to his library."

His library? A guy she knew well enough to buy a personal, meaningful gift? He supposed he shouldn't feel jealous. Sara obviously made friends wherever she went. In fact, she selected a few more purchases as they went along, all of them gifts for friends, some she intended to hoard until a birthday came along months down the line.

He didn't even know his friends' birthdays. For that matter, he didn't have that many friends. Except for Cooper and Max, who dragged him out for a beer or a hamburger every so often, he didn't socialize that much for the reasons he'd mentioned the night before—crowds, noise and meeting new people weren't on his list of favorite things.

Reece figured they had time for one more shop before they had to head for the hospital in Corpus. It was a dusty, cramped cubbyhole of a store, the merchandise piled so haphazardly he didn't hold high hopes.

Until he saw them, stacked in a box in a corner.

"Yes!" Sara, who had also spied the prize, dropped to her knees beside the box. "Look at them all. And they're in good condition!"

Reece was awash in relief. He'd been dreading confessing the dishwasher mishap to Miss Greer, of seeing the hurt and disappointment in the normally formidable woman's eyes.

He pulled the list from the back pocket of his jeans, joining Sara on the floor so they could sort through them.

"Even the teacups are in good shape," Sara said, examining a cup she had just unwrapped from a nest of tissue paper. "I can't believe we're so lucky."

The proprietress, a sixtyish woman with hair an improbable shade of red styled into a bird's nest, saw their interest and came over. "Hello, Sara. Aren't those lovely? I just got them in. Extremely rare, you know."

Reece thought the box had probably been sitting there for months, since it was covered with the same dust that coated everything else around it. But he wasn't going to argue.

"How much are they?" Reece asked. "I need three dinner plates, five—"

"I can't break up the set," the woman said. "The whole box will cost you four hundred."

Sara looked up, horrified. "Fiona. Four hundred?"

"I've got to make a profit, dear heart," the woman named Fiona said, sounding almost ashamed.

Reece was considered a skillful negotiator. When it came to shaving a few thousand dollars off the price of company assets or an office building, he usually prevailed. Even Max had been impressed with the way he'd negotiated for his car. He wasn't going to be taken in by one crafty old lady.

"I'm willing to go two hundred," Reece said.

"I can't let them go for less than three," Fiona said apologetically.

Reece pretended to consider. "I could do two twenty-five."

"Two fifty," Fiona said, looking pained.

"Deal. If you'll wrap the dishes securely, I'll pick them up tomorrow." He picked up the box and carried it to the front desk.

Fiona gleefully snatched Reece's platinum Visa from his hand.

Sara stood next to him, looking as if she wanted to explode as he completed the transaction. Only when they were outside did she speak again.

"I can't believe you were so cheap," she said.

"Listen, I'd let Miss Greer verbally flail me for weeks before I'd pay four hundred dollars for a box of old dishes. Fiona knew we were desperate. She must have heard us talking."

"But you heard her. She has to make a living."

"She probably paid twenty dollars for those, if that. The way she came down on the price so quickly means she had lots of wiggle room. Dealers expect you to counteroffer, especially the ones who quote you prices out of thin air."

"It hardly seems fair."

Reece had noticed that Sara didn't dicker over prices at all. The dealers around there probably rejoiced when they saw her walk through their front door.

Another fundamental difference between himself and Sara, and another reason anything long-term with her was out of the question.

She let go of their argument quickly, though, and he appreciated that about her. She could never stay in a bad mood for long.

When they arrived at Miss Greer's room, they found she already had a visitor—a woman in her thirties with long blond hair in a ponytail. She was sitting in a chair next to the elderly woman's bed, holding her hand.

She had the look of money about her—designer clothes, expertly cut and highlighted hair, sedate gold jewelry.

Miss Greer looked up when they entered, surprise and something else—something furtive—registering on her face. "I didn't think you were coming today."

"I know it's later than usual," Sara said apologetically as she approached the bed and kissed Miss Greer on her wrinkly cheek. She gave the other woman a curious look.

The blond woman stood. "Hi, I'm Valerie."

Sara held out her hand. "I'm Sara. I work at Miss Greer's bed-and-breakfast."

Valerie smiled. "She mentioned you, how helpful you've been." But Valerie didn't offer any further clues to her identity. She exchanged a look with Miss Greer that Reece couldn't interpret. "I think I'll, um, stretch my legs," Valerie said, "and give you all a chance to visit."

When she was gone, Sara took the chair Valerie had abandoned. Reece said hello, then pulled up another chair. An awkward silence descended, punctuated only by hisses of Miss Greer's roommate's oxygen.

"How do you know Valerie?" Sara asked casually. "I don't believe I've met her."

"She's not from around here," Miss Greer said

uneasily. "She's from Michigan. She's, um, well, she's my granddaughter."

Sara gaped like a landed fish, and Reece was shocked himself. He thought Miss Greer had never married.

"I had a child when I was twenty," she explained. "Nowadays it's no big deal, but back then it was scandalous to be pregnant without a husband. I went to a home, and I gave the child up for adoption. A few months ago she located me. She said she'd been searching for years."

"Oh, my goodness," Sara said.

"I wasn't sure if I wanted to meet her," Miss Greer said. "It was a painful chapter in my life, one I had put well behind me. But when I broke my hip, it occurred to me that I might not have that much time left. So I called Doreen—that's the name her adopted parents gave her—and told her I wanted to meet her, meet my grandchildren."

"That's wonderful." Sara's eyes swam with tears. "A whole family you never even knew about."

"I thought she would resent the fact I gave her away, but she apparently doesn't. She's coming for a visit with her whole family next month, but Valerie wanted to come right away. She's a physical therapist, you see, and she's between jobs, so it works out perfectly. She's going to stay at the B and B with me and get me back up to full speed."

"Wow. That's wonderful," Sara said again. "Is she nice? Do you like her?"

"Of course I like her!" Miss Greer said. "She's my granddaughter. Don't be impertinent. She's already talked to the doctor about my therapy, and we're all set. In fact, they're releasing me tomorrow since I'll have a qualified medical-type person to take care of me. I thought Valerie could stay in the Lilac Room. Can you make sure it's ready for her?"

"All the rooms are clean, Miss Greer," Sara said primly.

They talked about neutral subjects for a few minutes until Valerie returned bearing a fluffy blue fleece throw. "I saw this in the gift shop," she said cheerily. "You were complaining about your toes being cold, and I thought this was the perfect thing to wrap them in."

"How thoughtful!" Miss Greer said, greedy eyes on her granddaughter.

Reece and Sara stayed only a few more minutes. Valerie seemed a nice, friendly person, but Sara was less than her usual, effusive self. She was polite, but not overly much.

Finally she made up an excuse, and she and Reece left with Valerie's promise that she would bring her grandmother home tomorrow.

"Wow, what a story," Reece said as they waited for the elevator.

"Mmm-hmm."

"I never suspected Miss Greer as the type to have had an illicit affair in her youth. I wonder what happened to the baby's father, and why they didn't marry."

"Who knows? Already married, maybe. Or he might have just taken off. Men do that."

"Women do it, too." He thought about the possibility

of Sara taking off for her California movie job. Or a job on a cruise ship.

"Yeah, guess you're right," she said, sounding disturbingly glum. He wasn't used to that from her, and was further bothered when she didn't shake off her mood right away. She seemed unusually pensive, and he struggled to come up with a way to cheer her up.

His phone rang. He checked the caller ID and inwardly groaned. His father again, probably wanting to remind him for the tenth time about some meeting. He let the call roll over to voice mail.

"Don't you need to answer that?" Sara asked.

"Nah. Want to grab dinner?" Though they'd eaten a late lunch, he was hungry. "I'll take you out. I'll even let you pick the restaurant—anywhere you want." God help his stomach.

"I'm not really that hungry."

Okay, now he knew something was really wrong. "Sara," he said, carefully, after they'd settled in his car, "I don't want to pry, but you seem a little upset by Miss Greer's news. Aren't you happy for her?"

"Well, of course I'm happy for her. How lovely to reunite with someone you thought lost to you forever, especially for someone like Miss Greer, who believed she had no family at all." She looked at Reece, blinking a little sheepishly. "It's just that I was looking forward to playing nurse for Miss Greer."

"You feel Valerie is taking your place?"

She put a hand to her forehead. "It's silly, I know."

He didn't think it was silly. She'd been the most important person in her employer's life for a lot of years.

Having someone else burst onto the scene and shove you aside—not that Valerie had any idea that was what she was doing—must have left Sara feeling adrift.

"She probably can't cook like you," Reece pointed out. "You'll still need to help run the bed-and-breakfast."

"And what about you?" she said.

A very good question. Once Miss Greer was at home she could probably handle reservations and money just fine. Now that she'd cut down on the pain meds, she wasn't suffering from any cognitive difficulties. Furthermore, Allie and Cooper had their business finances completely under control. Everything was on computer; Allie understood the bookkeeping program and had no problems with it. Loans had been paid off; taxes were up-to-date.

Then there was his real job. He still had tons of vacation time left, but that didn't mean he could extend his leave of absence indefinitely. He had responsibilities back home, people depending on him. His father's and brother's daily phone calls had become much more uncomfortable during the past week as they pressured him to return home.

Reece had no good reason to remain in Port Clara. Except for the one sitting in his passenger seat, waiting for him to answer. And he had no idea how long she'd even be here.

"I can't stay," he said, carefully watching her face.

She flinched. She actually recoiled from his statement. But she quickly recovered. "I know. But what about the wedding?"

He'd nearly forgotten. Cooper would never forgive him if he missed that—he was the best man. "That's not for two weeks. Don't worry, I'll be there. But I have to attend a key meeting next week. In fact, I have to fly home tomorrow to prepare for it." If he made a serious effort to soothe ruffled feathers and put out fires once he got home, his father would be placated.

He hoped.

Contrary to what Sara thought, his father *would* fire him if he believed Reece was shirking responsibilities or acting in a way that didn't serve Remington Industries' best interests.

"Tomorrow. You're leaving tomorrow?" Sara looked distressed at the thought.

"I wish I didn't have to." He reached over and stroked her bare arm.

"You don't *have* to," she said. "You're an adult with a free will. You can do anything you want with your life."

"Sara, I can't leave my job. The company was founded by my great-grandfather. I've worked there my whole adult life. I have family there, a home."

"But do you *like* your job? Do you enjoy it?"

"I know you find this hard to believe, but I do. Yes, it's stressful, having responsibility for all that money, the long hours, the deadlines. But I love it."

Then why, just now as he'd thought about it, did his stomach give him that painful twinge? His ulcer, which was supposed to be cured, had bothered him very little since he'd been down here, he realized.

The twinge was followed by a sharp pain in his chest.

What the hell was that? But after a few moments the pain eased, and he dismissed it.

"How will you get your car home?" she asked.

He'd been thinking about that. "Maybe I'll sell it."

"Oh, no. It's such a nice car. Well, it was before I wrecked it." She ran one hand along the burled-wood dashboard, then briefly touched the gearshift knob. "Besides, you look sexy behind the wheel."

"Hmm." Reason enough to keep the car. "I'll think about it."

"I could drive it to New York for you."

Only if he lost his mind. "Mmm-hmm," he said noncommittally.

"I'll drive slow as my grandmother."

"I know." But he could just imagine what kind of trouble Sara would get into driving across the country by herself. She couldn't even read a map!

"I probably couldn't do it anyway." She heaved a resigned sigh. "I can't leave Miss Greer in the lurch. Valerie can't do it all."

Which brought them back to their original discussion. "So, see, she does need you, and you can stop looking so glum."

Sara smiled, and this time it seemed sincere. "I can pick any restaurant, huh?"

"That's what I said, all right."

"I know of this Lithuanian place—" She cut herself off, laughing. "You should see the look on your face. Just kidding. How about Italian?"

Italian seemed a reasonable compromise between her yearning for something exotic and his desire for the familiar. He doubted, though, that any compromise could bridge their other differences. The gap between them was as big as the Grand Canyon.

Chapter Ten

Sara had known all along Reece would be leaving, but when he actually started packing, she found it hard not to cry.

They had spent last night together, and again she had lost count of how many times they'd made love. Now that they were getting used to each other, their lovemaking had become much more adventurous. Reece might be conservative and set in his ways in the rest of his life, but in the bedroom he was passionate and inventive.

He'd spoiled her. She couldn't imagine anyone else would ever compare.

Cooper was driving Reece to the airport for an evening flight into JFK. Reece had asked Sara if she wanted to ride along, but she claimed she was too busy. The truth was, she didn't want to prolong saying goodbye. She didn't want to embarrass either one of them by weeping in front of his cousin, and she doubted Reece would kiss her goodbye when Cooper was there.

"I think I've got everything," he said when she met

him in the hall. He had two large rolling suitcases and a small carry-on. She offered to carry the small bag down for him, not that he couldn't easily do it himself, but she wanted to make herself useful, give her a reason for being there.

He let her.

"I think I heard Cooper's car drive up," he said just as the doorbell rang.

"Evidently."

"Sure you won't come to the airport?" he said as he trotted down the stairs, easily carrying the two heavy-looking cases.

"No, um, I've got a cake in the oven." Lame excuse.

He paused at the front door and, before opening it, slid his hand under Sara's hair to the back of her neck and pulled her close for a kiss.

A rather perfunctory kiss.

He opened the door. "Hey, Cooper," she said.

Cooper grabbed one of the suitcases. "We better move or we'll get held up at the ferry. It's crowded this time of day."

"Yeah, I'm coming." Then he turned to Sara. "I almost forgot." He reached into his pocket and handed her his car keys. "With all the wedding preparations, you might need a car. You can use mine while I'm gone."

She took the keys. "Thanks. That's generous."

He further surprised her by taking the carry-on bag from her, setting it down, then sweeping her into his arms for a proper kiss. Or an improper one, depending on your point of view.

"I'll be back soon."

She nodded, unable to speak. Yes, he would be back. But then what?

Nothing, she answered herself. She'd been an idiot to form an attachment with a man whose view of life was so different from her own.

As he carried his bags down the front porch steps, she saw Cooper watching, obviously surprised by what he'd seen.

Rather than stand on the porch like a lovesick puppy, watching as the taillights of Cooper's BMW disappeared down the street, she slipped inside.

Maybe she would see about that cake—for real. Other than cleaning Reece's room and readying it for the next guests, she didn't have much to do.

Valerie had brought Miss Greer home that afternoon and gotten herself and her grandmother settled into their respective rooms. She would handle all aspects of the older woman's care, from therapy to medications to meals.

Sara discovered the part about meals as she entered the kitchen and found Valerie preparing some chicken breasts for the oven—and looking right at home.

"I hope you don't mind," Valerie said, "but Grandma was hungry. I'm making enough for all of us."

"Oh. Thanks. Please feel free to make yourself at home. Anything you need, just ask."

Valerie smiled. "Thanks."

Petty as it was, Sara wanted to dislike the woman. But Valerie was friendly, respectful of Sara's role—and very efficient. Sara would still be required to fix breakfast and handle the housekeeping, but all else was under control.

She tried to tell herself this was a good thing. She had a wedding to cater. But she had a hard time focusing on her friend's wedded bliss when she'd never felt so alone in her life.

"WHAT WAS *THAT?*" Cooper asked the moment they were in the car with the doors closed.

"What?" Reece asked innocently.

"That kiss!"

"Oh. Sara and I…" What? Spent a couple of nights together having the most incredible sex of his life? "I thought this would be old news by now. We went to that party together."

"Allie said she thought something was going on with you two, but I honestly didn't believe her."

Reece sat up straighter. "Why not? You think I'm not good enough for her?"

Cooper looked over at him as if he'd just ordered squid at a restaurant. "Why would you even think that? Of course I don't believe that. I just can't see the two of you together."

"Why not?"

"Do I have to spell it out? She's such a free spirit. I mean, her lifestyle is…"

"There's nothing wrong with her lifestyle. She lives life on her terms, and I like that about her."

"I wasn't criticizing. I just didn't think she would appeal to you. Yeah, she's not bad-looking—"

"Are you kidding? She's the most gorgeous woman I ever saw. Have you even looked at her?"

Cooper laughed. "Easy, buckaroo. I've been too busy

looking at my own woman to pay much attention to yours. Is she? Your woman, I mean."

Reece sighed. "I wish. I really like her. I like being with her. But, damn it, you're right. There's no way we could work this thing out."

"Unless you resign from Remington Industries and relocate down here."

"Exactly. It's impossible."

"I was making a practical suggestion. Resign. Max and I resigned because we were so overshadowed by our older brothers, and I know your situation is similar. Unless you *like* playing second banana to Bret?"

"I like my job," he said through gritted teeth, though his stomach twinged again.

"You're a bean counter. You could do that anywhere."

"I could never match the salary I'm making at another company, and you know it. It's taken me years to get where I am. Not to mention, the company needs me."

"First off, you don't need that much money. You don't spend half of what you make. Second, if you put yourself out there, you could probably get a job as a CFO at a decent-size company where you'd make decent money and get a little respect. You're not just a bean counter, you're an incredibly good one. Let Max put your résumé together."

Reece rubbed his stomach. "Can we not talk about this?"

Cooper shrugged. "Fine. But speaking as one who recently found a woman to spend the rest of my life with, and having overcome some pretty steep odds to make it work, I just want to say that it's worth it. If you've fallen in love with Sara—and I hear it in your voice that you have—don't give her up for a stupid job."

Love? Who said anything about love?

"I'm not in love with Sara," Reece said fiercely. "Anyway, we're too different. Everybody can see that. You and Allie have the same values—you love sailing and fishing. You both loved and respected Uncle Johnny. Sara and I see eye to eye on almost nothing."

"Okay, fine."

They hardly spoke the rest of the way to the airport. But Reece continued to think about Sara as the miles between them grew, and he anticipated with dread what awaited him back at his office.

The thoughts he entertained were not those of a man who loves his job.

ARCHIBALD REMINGTON III, chief financial officer of Remington Industries, entered the conference room and assumed his seat at the head of the table like a king ascending the throne. He eyed each person at the table in turn, his gaze finally resting on Reece.

Reece had been back for a week, but Archie hadn't offered any welcome home or asked how things were in Port Clara. But that was normal for Reece's father. He was a no-nonsense, cut-to-the-chase kind of guy.

Reece used to aspire to be just like him. His father was one of the most respected businessmen in the country. He had shepherded the company's finances toward ever-increasing profits even when the economy turned down.

Today, however, Reece looked at his father with new eyes and realized he didn't want to be like him after all. The man had his good qualities, but compassion, empathy and any ability to have fun weren't among them.

Reece's father called the meeting to order. The purpose of the meeting was so Bret could present a financial overview of a company Remington Industries was interested in acquiring. Reece had actually done most of the work—long-distance from Port Clara—but Bret was far better at public speaking than Reece, so he normally was in charge of presenting their findings to the board of directors.

Reece had to admit, the PowerPoint presentation was slick. But when board members started asking questions, Bret often floundered and Reece had to step in and clarify.

When it was over, Archie congratulated Bret on a job well done. He said nothing to his younger son, which irked Reece more today than it usually did, especially because he knew his father would be retiring in a few months and the board would have to name his replacement. Archie made no secret that he wanted Bret to step into his shoes, and he was doing his best to present his eldest son in the most favorable light.

"We'll reconvene next Monday, one week from today, at 10:00 a.m.," Archie said as everyone stood and gathered their things.

"I won't be here next Monday," Reece said.

Archie went still, looking at him with razor-sharp eyes. "Excuse me?"

"Cooper's wedding is next weekend. Afterward I'm

driving my car up from Texas. I won't be back till Thursday next week."

"After a month of vacation, you're leaving again? Hire someone to drive your car. You're needed here."

Reece knew that was the more practical decision.

Bret and Reece walked down the hallway together toward their offices. "Thanks for saving my bacon," Bret said in a low voice. "If Dad knew how much you covered for me, he wouldn't even think of promoting me higher."

"I don't cover for you," Reece said, sort of meaning it. "We each have our strengths. You can do the CFO job so long as you recognize where you need help, and surround yourself with people who can fill in the gaps."

"You'll be right there with me, you know. You've pushed me most of the way up the corporate ladder— I'm not going to the top without you. The first thing I'll do if I get the job is give you a better title and a whopping big raise."

They had reached Reece's office, which was half the size of Bret's down the hall and in bad need of a paint job.

"And a better office," Bret said, looking around.

Reece just shook his head. "I'm happy where I am." Or maybe he'd gotten complacent with his mediocre position. "Hey, are you going to Cooper's wedding?"

"I wanted to. But Dad scheduled a golf game for Saturday with some bigwig hotel owner. Command performance. He's trotting me around introducing me to everyone like a damn show dog."

Reece couldn't blame Bret for choosing the golf game over the wedding. He had a lot more at stake than Reece did.

Reece looked grimly at the stack of paper waiting for him in his in-box. "Guess I better get to work."

SARA THREW herself into the last-minute wedding plans, grateful that Reece had left his car, because it turned out she really needed one. She was going to have to do something about her transportation problem soon.

"I can't believe Reece left his car for you to drive," Allie commented as they drove back to the B and B, the Mercedes's trunk filled with all the ingredients Sara needed to make the lavish Mexican buffet planned for her friend's wedding. "I think the boy is smitten. Men typically don't let women drive their expensive sports cars after they wreck them."

"The wreck wasn't my fault. And Reece isn't smitten. If he were, he would still be here."

"Oh, Sara. He can't just abandon his job. That would be irresponsible, and we both know Reece is anything but irresponsible."

"But shouldn't love be more important?"

Allie made a frustrated noise. "It's not that simple. Let's turn it around. Say you'd been the one on vacation, and you'd met Reece in New York. Would you have just stayed there, abandoning Miss Greer without a second thought?"

Sara took a few moments to think about her answer. "No, I guess I wouldn't. But Reece hasn't asked me to come to New York, so it's a moot point."

"What if he wanted you to go there, and stay there?"

"I've done stupider things for a guy. Yeah, I think I would do it."

"I thought you only liked big cities to visit."

She shrugged. "I could be persuaded to change my mind. But I would make sure Miss Greer was taken care of. I'd find someone good to take my place."

"So maybe Reece has to take care of things back home. Give him time to miss you. If it was meant to be, you'll find a way."

They arrived back at the Sunsetter, and Sara immediately got to work mixing the masa harina for homemade corn tortillas.

"So what should I do when I see him?" Sara asked. She hadn't felt this insecure about a guy since…well, she never had. Even when she was a teenager she hadn't angsted about guys.

"Make your feelings known. Do you love him?"

"Yes, I think so," Sara said miserably. "I think about him all the time. I fantasize about being with him. I picture what our children would look like."

Allie smiled. "Sounds like love to me. Could you commit to him? As in, the rest of your life?"

Sara couldn't answer that question quite so easily. "The rest of my life is a very long time."

"So you're asking Reece to give up everything he knows, everything that's familiar—including his family and a six-figure income—to hang out with you for as long as it lasts? Think about it."

Sara didn't have to think about it long. Reece was a man uncomfortable with uncertainty. If he made a major life change, he wouldn't do so unless he was able to map out the next fifty years. Sara, on the other hand, had never been able to commit to anything—not a job, not a man, not even a hairstyle. Once, when she was a little girl, her mother had made her cut her hair for a swim class at the Y. She had cried for a week because she'd been forced to wear her hair the same way every single day until it grew out.

She'd been expecting Reece to live life the way she did. If she saw something she wanted, she went for it and worried later about all the consequences. He could never conduct his life that way and maintain his identity.

"Are you thinking?" Allie asked. "Or have you tuned me out?"

"I'm thinking." And she was trying not to cry. She'd been doing that a lot lately. Who knew falling in love could be so painful?

REECE LANDED at the Corpus Christi airport at eleven o'clock Saturday morning on Cooper's wedding day, two hours before the actual ceremony.

"You're cutting it close," Max said as Reece climbed into his cousin's red Corvette outside the baggage claim.

"I know. I had a meeting Friday afternoon that lasted for hours and I missed my original flight. This was the best I could do on short notice. You have the tux?"

"I have the tux."

"How did the rehearsal go?"

"We didn't really have a rehearsal. We just had a big party on the private deck at Old Salt's Bar and Grill."

"Was Sara there?"

Max snorted. "Of course. She's Allie's maid of honor."

"Did she have a date?"

"No…" Max flashed a sly smile. "Oh, yeah. I heard about you and the flower child. Bit out of your league, wouldn't you say?"

At least Max didn't mince words the way Cooper had. Cooper, being older, had been protective toward Reece when they were growing up, an attitude that lingered into adulthood. Max, who was younger, had been the one to tease, though in a good-natured way. He still did.

"She's so completely out of my league," Reece said glumly.

"Aw, now, don't be like that. I just meant she's different from the type of girl you usually date. When you date."

"I know." Which was why he should cut it off clean. Cooper, who would soon be on his honeymoon piloting the *Dragonfly* down to Mexico, had offered to let Reece stay at his house, and he'd accepted. Because he knew that if he stayed at the Sunsetter, he and Sara would most likely end up in bed, and leaving Sunday would be twice as hard as the last time he'd left, because he knew he wasn't returning.

The next couple of hours were filled with frenzied activity at Cooper's house as they all got ready for the wedding. However, Cooper, Max and Reece did find time for a private toast with a very good Scotch Cooper had been saving for whenever the first one of them got married.

"Well, this is it, guys," Cooper said. "The end of the Three Musketeers. I'll be married, and Reece will be half a country away."

"We'll still see each other," Reece argued. He was

happy for Cooper, happy that his two cousins had made the leap away from Remington Industries, where their older brothers would forever have prevented them from reaching the peak of their professions.

But he hated thinking about being the sole survivor at the family company, without the other musketeers for support.

When it came right down to it, he didn't like change.

"Yeah," Max said, "but it won't be the same. Once or twice a year at Christmas or Thanksgiving…"

"Hey, let's not get maudlin," Cooper said. "I'm getting married. Wish me well."

They drank a toast to the groom, and to the bride, and it was only after Reece had drained his glass did he remember that he wasn't supposed to drink with his seasick medicine, which he hadn't yet taken.

Chapter Eleven

The *Clifford's Landing Party Barge* was decked out with so much white ribbon, lace and flowers, it looked like a wedding cake.

Sara wanted to be happy and excited for her best friend, and she was. But she now had something else to worry about.

For some unknown reason, she'd looked at her calendar this morning, and she'd realized something. She was late. As in, really, really late. And the thought had occurred to her that she just might be pregnant. Yes, she was on birth control pills, but sometimes she forgot to take them.

Reece would freak out. Truth be told, *she* was freaking out a little. She'd run to the closest drugstore and bought a pregnancy test, but she didn't have the time—or the courage—to take it now. She resolved to put the problem out of her mind, at least for today, Allie's day.

Sara was pleased with how her very first wedding catering job was going. She'd timed her preparations of the various dishes to perfection. Now, as the hour for departure approached, guests were boarding and Sara was putting the finishing touches on the hot dishes.

Valerie had offered to assist, and Miss Greer, whose recovery was going so well it shocked everyone including her doctor, had insisted she could manage on her own for a couple of hours so that Valerie could help serve and watch over the buffet while Sara did her maid-of-honor duties.

"We're good here," Valerie said. "You go help the bride."

When Sara entered the salon, which had become the impromptu bride's room, her breath caught in her throat at the sight of tomboy Allie in her girlie-girl wedding gown.

"Oh, Allie, you look like a princess."

"Princess for a day. Every bride is entitled."

Sara wondered if she would ever get to be a princess. Thinking about Allie sharing her life with Cooper, having kids, growing old with him—she had to admit it held some attraction. Maybe it was the shock of a possible pregnancy, but she was starting to realize her free-spirit lifestyle couldn't last forever. Sooner or later she would have to decide who she wanted to be. If she was soon to be a mother…oh, Lord…she would have to be a responsible one.

Since Allie's parents were deceased, Cooper's mother had stepped into the role of helping the bride get ready. She also fussed with Sara's hair, which she'd wound on top of her head and woven with flowers, then powdered her nose and called it good. Jane, who lived on the boat next door to Allie's *Dragonfly,* was a bridesmaid, but she evidently didn't need any help in the primping department. She looked as if she'd just stepped off the pages of *Vogue,* and the raw silk dress she'd chosen clung to her size-two figure, making Sara feel like a horse by comparison.

Jane's three-year-old daughter, Kaylee, was there, too. She was Allie's flower girl, and though she was opposite Jane in her coloring with her bright blond curls, she was every bit as beautiful.

"I think we're ready," Mrs. Remington declared. "I'll cue the musicians to begin, then I'll go stand with Jonathan, and we can start. Good luck, dear. You'll need it, being Cooper's wife. He's so much like his father, even if he won't admit it."

Allie laughed nervously after her future mother-in-law left. "Cooper would deny that to his grave, but after seeing him together with his dad, the comparison is obvious."

The trio of musicians started the processional song.

Sara swallowed back the tears that threatened. Honestly, she cried over anything these days. Did pregnancy hormones make you more emotional? But her best friend getting married was a good thing to cry over.

"I don't know when I'll have a chance to say so again," Allie said quickly, "but thank you both for being my friends. You're the best friends anyone could wish for."

"Allie," Jane said in a scolding voice, "you promised not to make me cry until after the ceremony. My makeup is going to run."

They all drew close for one last hug, and then it was time. As the boat cut smoothly through the water, Jane went first down the makeshift aisle among the guests. Most were standing, as there were only a few places to sit. Then Sara went. As she approached the front of the boat, she got her first glimpse of Reece since his return from New York. Oh, God, did he look handsome in a tux.

He also looked tense, as he had when he'd first arrived. Less than two weeks back at his job had undone two months of beach life. She wished he could see what the stress was doing to him.

He was watching her, too, and as she reached the place where she guessed she was supposed to stand, he gave her a little finger wave. She winked at him in answer, and she could have sworn he blushed.

Little Kaylee trotted down the aisle next, flinging rose petals with great glee. Then all eyes were on the bride as she made her appearance. Not a princess, Sara decided. An angel. Her friend had never looked so radiant.

The ceremony was short and sweet, the bride and groom exchanging vows with strong, confident voices. They obviously had no qualms about pledging the rest of their lives. Was something wrong with her? Sara wondered. Didn't most women look forward to the day when they could settle down, maybe have kids and a dog and a house in the suburbs?

Sara's attention drifted to Reece again. He was watching his cousin with obvious fondness, but he also appeared solemn. This was serious stuff to Reece. Allie was right about that. He wasn't going to rearrange his whole life on a lark.

The bride and groom kissed, a long, slow, slightly inappropriate embrace, and everyone cheered. The happy couple paraded down the aisle arm in arm. Then suddenly Reece was there, offering his arm to Sara.

"You look beautiful," he said in a low voice. "I don't know why anyone looked at the bride when you were standing next to her."

Now Sara felt herself blushing. She looped her arm in his and they followed the bride and groom. Max and Jane fell into step behind them, with Kylie holding on to the hem of her mother's dress, having forgotten her flower duties.

Cooper and Allie paused once they cleared the crowd. "We'd like to invite everyone to enjoy the Mexican buffet provided by our talented bridesmaid, Sara Kaufman."

That was Sara's cue to hurry back to her catering duties, or Valerie would quickly be overwhelmed. She reluctantly released her handsome groomsman. "Save me a dance, huh?"

He frowned. "Uh, yeah."

What was that about? Was he wishing he'd never hooked up with her? Embarrassed that a few people had identified them as a couple? Now that he'd spent some time back in his regular life, maybe his dalliance with that crazy bed-and-breakfast girl seemed frivolous, even foolish and low class.

Despite the fact they were on a boat, Sara had rented good china dishes and fancy silverware. She risked some of it going overboard, but that was better than leaving a trail of paper plates fouling up the ocean, which was exactly what would have happened in the stiff breeze.

The guests lined up to sample Sara's buffet, which pleased her no end. She liked nothing better than to feed people food they loved. This was much more fun than catering a movie set, where the people she served were so absorbed in their work that she was invisible.

Here, among the people of Port Clara whom she'd come to know over the past ten-plus years, she was loved and appreciated. She knew most of the guests—at least the ones who weren't Cooper's out-of-town friends and family—and every one of them had a kind greeting.

The one person she wanted to see, though, was conspicuously avoiding her. He was busy with the photographer, posing with his cousins and the bride and looking kind of miserable, even when he smiled.

Once the main rush of guests had gone through the buffet line, Allie dragged Sara out from behind the table for pictures of their own. Allie certainly would have an interesting wedding album, with the boat and the ocean as backdrops for all the photos.

Sara posed with Allie, then with Allie, Jane and Kaylee. Then the men joined them. Reece stood beside her, his arm slipped around her waist in a distinctly nonsexual fashion, and she knew she was right. He regretted getting intimate with her and was trying to extricate himself gracefully. Visions of the reunion sex she'd planned for tonight faded away. Maybe she would just get drunk at the beach party instead.

No, scratch that. She couldn't drink until she knew for certain she wasn't pregnant.

Reece released her the moment the photographer

had the shots he wanted, then wandered away to stand by the railing, all alone.

"Poor Reece," she heard Allie saying to Cooper.

Poor Reece? What about poor Sara? She was the one feeling unappreciated at the moment.

"You never should have let him drink that Scotch," Allie said, scolding her new husband.

"How was I supposed to know he wouldn't be able to take his Dramamine if he drank alcohol?"

Sara gasped. Reece wasn't being cranky and distant on purpose. He was seasick.

With no worries about her pride now, she went straight to him. "Reece?"

He turned, seeming surprised to see her. His complexion was definitely greenish. "Sara. Hi."

"Don't look at me, look at the horizon," she said. "I've heard it helps."

He complied. "So I haven't done a very good job disguising my delicate condition, eh?"

"I heard Allie and Cooper talking. I'm sorry you're not feeling well."

"It could be worse. At least I'm not hurling."

"Maybe you would feel better if you ate something."

If anything, he turned greener. "Ah, no. I don't think Mexican food is the answer."

"But I made you up a special enchilada. No peppers, no spices, nothing weird."

"Can we not talk about food?"

Oh, dear. He really was in a bad way. "Here, give me your hand." She urged him to release his death grip on the railing. She loved his hands. Big, strong, capable hands, not like those she expected to find attached to an accountant. She flipped his hand over and began a slow massage of the inside of his wrist, digging her thumbs in with no small amount of pressure as she moved them in circles.

"What are you doing?"

"This is an acupressure point for motion sickness," she explained. "This really works. And if it doesn't, well, I'll just kiss you until you've forgotten you're on a boat."

He turned to look at her, obviously surprised by her boldness.

"Keep looking at the horizon. Take long, slow breaths."

SARA'S TREATMENT seemed to be working. He shouldn't be surprised; she'd cured a headache with nothing but her talented hands.

After a couple of minutes of the soothing massage, keeping his gaze focused into the distance like she said and breathing in big lungfuls of fresh sea air, the dizziness began to fade. Maybe the acupressure point really did work. Or maybe it was the fact that Sara touching him anywhere on his body focused his attention, and his blood circulation, well below his head or his stomach.

"The cruise is almost over," Sara said soothingly.

Strangely, Reece suddenly wasn't anxious to be back on dry land. He actually found it pleasant, standing here with Sara's warm, curvy body beside him, her soft voice lulling him.

"Any better?" she asked. "You've got more color in your face."

"Actually, yes. A lot better." He slipped an arm

around her. "Thanks, Dr. Sara. I don't believe I've properly greeted you."

She looked up at him with a warm smile just for him, her lips moist and rosy, the afternoon sun kissing her face and accentuating the slight dusting of freckles across her nose, and all his plans to make a clean break fell overboard. He swooped down for a kiss that felt like coming home. He didn't care that half the wedding guests were gawking at them, or that word would surely get back to his father, who would quickly conclude— correctly—that Sara was the reason he'd been in no hurry to return home.

His father could rave and criticize and belittle all he wanted when Reece got back home. His family and the company would have him for the rest of his life. But Sara had him for this weekend.

She'd made him a special enchilada. How sweet was that?

The party barge beached itself on a long stretch of sand adjacent to the Port Clara Country Club. And while it wasn't closed off to the public, once the wedding guests had disembarked the boat and more had arrived by land, Cooper and Allie pretty much owned the beach.

Sara and Valerie had to stay behind to break down the buffet and pack up the leftovers, but Sara urged Reece to get his feet back on solid ground. "This won't take long. I'll rejoin the party shortly."

"It won't be a party without you."

He disembarked with her smile on his mind. If he'd known this was how to cure seasickness, he would have thrown away his Dramamine long ago. Still, he was grateful to reach the end of the gangway and feel the sand beneath his feet. Until the first person to greet him was his uncle Jonathan, Cooper's father and VP of Legal Affairs at Remington Industries.

Jonathan shook hands with a crushing grip, pumping Reece's arm so hard he thought his head might fall off. "Reece. Glad you made it on time. I guess my brother made you miss your plane."

"The meeting ran long, sir," Reece said diplomatically, although at the time he had wondered if his father was deliberately pontificating in the most long-winded way possible, hoping to cause Reece to miss his flight. He'd never thought of his dad as being passive-aggressive before, but maybe he simply hadn't seen it.

"So," Jonathan continued as they made their way toward the tent where the cake was set up at one end and a bartender at the other. "Who's the girl you were locking lips with?"

Reece was prepared for the question. "Sara. She helps run the bed-and-breakfast where we all stayed when we first came down."

Jonathan raised an eyebrow. "She carries hospitality a little far, don't you think?"

Reece didn't honor the question with an answer.

"You're not serious about her, are you?"

"No," he said automatically, but immediately knew he was lying. No matter how unlikely a future with Sara was, what he felt for her could not be labeled trivial. "But I could be. Why, is something wrong with her?"

"I'm sure she's a very nice girl." Nice being code for *fine for someone else, but not for a Remington.*

"Dad." Cooper had appeared beside them. "Stop torturing Reece. I want you to meet some friends of mine from the Gulf Coast Yacht Club. You've been talking about buying a yacht and sailing around the world when you retire, right?"

Jonathan's interest was instantly diverted and he happily trotted off after his son.

Now that he was on firm ground, Reece was ravenous. He again thought of the special enchilada Sara had prepared for him and wished he'd been able to take advantage of her thoughtfulness. But he suspected more food would soon be available. Already, people were building fires and breaking out the hamburgers and hot dogs. The party looked to be shaping up as similar to the last beach party he'd attended, though he doubted any party could top that one.

His gaze strayed toward the barge, but he saw no sign of Sara.

"She'll be along." It was Allie, who had already ditched her veil. The hem of her long, white dress was hitched up and fastened at her hip with some elaborate device so she wouldn't get it dirty in the sand, and she was barefoot.

"Who?" Reece asked, embarrassed that he was so transparent.

Allie rolled her eyes. "Give me a break. You can dance with me until she shows up."

"Aren't you supposed to be dancing with Cooper? I mean, isn't that traditional?"

"Has anything about this wedding been traditional yet? He's busy talking boats with rich old men. And to think I was once worried about ever finding a man who loved sailing as much as I do." While she talked, she dragged Reece toward a group that was already dancing. He didn't want to be rude, but he had no interest in dancing with anyone but Sara. He smiled just remembering how she'd put her bare feet on top of his shoes.

"So how long are you staying in Port C?" Allie asked.

"I'm flying back Sunday night." And praying he wouldn't suffer any delays, because he was cutting it close to make the crucial Monday-morning meeting.

"Oh." She sounded disappointed. "I thought you'd stay longer."

"Allie, I stayed down here for more than a month."

"I know, but…Cooper and Max are really bummed you won't move down here. They were hoping once you were here you would have so much fun you would change your mind."

"What would I do down here? I have to earn a living."

"Open your own accounting firm. The way you organized our finances was amazing. A lot of businesses would pay to have you do the same."

"Allie, I can't. Is this about Sara?"

She looked guilty. "Maybe, partly. No one but me gives you and Sara a snowball's chance in hell, but I can see something there. Don't you want to prove them wrong?"

"So now we've become the object of gossip?"

"Just among the people who care about you. Everybody wants you to be happy."

"What makes you think I'm not happy?"

"Oh, I don't know. It might be that tense, worried look on your face every time you mention your work."

Really? "I love my job." How many times did he have to explain that to people?

The twinge in his stomach stopped him for a second, though. Who was he trying to convince—them or himself? No, no, no, he wasn't going to let his feelings for Sara cloud his judgment. Yes, he was crazy about her. Yes, he wished there was some way they could be together, at least long enough to find out if their attraction was more than a flash in the pan. But there wasn't.

Even if Sara wanted to relocate to New York, what if she didn't like it? Once she'd gotten her fill of ethnic restaurants, not to mention snow and icy wind, would she get restless and take off? She had chosen warm, sleepy Port Clara as a home base for a reason.

Allie didn't appear happy with him. "If you say so, Reece."

As the song ended, Cooper appeared to reclaim the bride. His jacket and tie were gone, his shirt open and his sleeves rolled up. He didn't look quite as happy and carefree as a new bridegroom should.

"Have you guys seen a weather report lately?"

Allie looked surprised by the question. "I've been a little busy getting married."

"I'm sorry, sweetheart, but we're going to have to delay our honeymoon."

"What? Why?"

"Because of the hurricane."

Chapter Twelve

Sara finally gave up waiting for Reece to find her; she went in search of him. She found him a few minutes later, talking with the bride and groom—and all of them looked worried.

"Hey, what's going on?" she asked. "Did somebody die?"

"Hey, Sara," Reece said, managing a tense smile. "No one died. But there's a hurricane."

"Oh, is that all?"

"Is that all?" Allie repeated. "Have you ever been through one?"

"Yes, and I don't mean to make light of it, but it's not a hurricane. It's an itty-bitty tropical storm, and they don't even know if it will hit here, or when. It could just peter out."

Reece looked relieved. "Have you seen a weather report?"

"Yes. Max checked it out on his super-duper phone. You guys are worrying for nothing." She took Reece's hand. "C'mon, Reece, let's dance."

THE OFFICIAL WEDDING reception lasted for a couple of hours, after which the bartender vanished and the tent came down. The bride and groom said their good-byes and left for their wedding night in some fancy hotel in Corpus. But the wedding revelers showed no signs of slowing down. The party would probably continue into the night, but for once Sara wasn't in a partying mood.

Her reunion with Reece hadn't gone at all as she'd planned. He'd been perfectly pleasant to her, solicitous, even. He'd fetched her a piece of wedding cake and a glass of champagne, which she'd covertly dumped in the sand. He'd danced with her, and he'd touched her often in a way that promised he hadn't lost interest.

But there was an edge to Reece, something on his mind that kept his forehead creased with worry. Maybe it was talk of the storm, or maybe it was something else.

The worst thing, though, was that she had no idea what his plans were for the evening—and whether they included her.

She would have to take the proverbial bull by the horns.

"So, Reece," she said, sitting in a folding chair next to him. "Have you had enough party?"

"I'm just waiting for Max. He's giving me a ride back to Cooper's house."

"Oh. Well, I'm heading back to the B and B. Do you want to come with me?"

"How? Isn't the car at the marina?"

"I planned ahead, aren't you proud of me? I parked the Benz in the lot just on the other side of those dunes."

She could see he was tempted, but for some reason he hesitated.

"Reece, what is it? Do you want to spend the night with me or not?"

"Of course I do."

"Then what is your problem?"

"The problem is…hell, the problem is I don't want to say goodbye to you. I don't want to get on a plane Sunday night and never see you again. And if we spend the rest of the weekend together, getting on that plane is just going to be ten times harder."

Sara smiled. She hadn't expected such a heartfelt confession. "So don't get on the plane."

When she saw the pained expression on his face, she wanted to take the words back. "No, forget I said that. I know it's not fair. I can't expect you to give up the life you've built in New York—I get that."

"I'm sorry, Sara. I wish things could work out. But we've both known, from the beginning, we're from different worlds."

She wanted to tell him what a cheap cop-out that was. Cooper and Allie were from the exact same different worlds that Reece and Sara were from, yet they were making it work. It was all about priorities, and clearly she wasn't that high on his list. But if they got into a big fight tonight, he would go back to New York mad at her, and that wasn't what she wanted.

She didn't want him to leave until she'd had a chance to take a pregnancy test. And if it was positive? Of course she had to tell him. And of course he would take responsibility. But she didn't want a baby to be the reason he stayed with her.

"So you're going to let what's coming Sunday night ruin the whole weekend?" At his questioning look, she took his hand. "We've found something special. Sometimes special things are, by nature, short-lived. Why ruin it by worrying about when it has to end?"

Finally he got it. He gave her a look that could melt cold steel and got to his feet, pulling her with him. "I can't argue with your logic. Let's get out of here."

Sara had never seen Reece drive as fast as he did that day. They didn't talk, perhaps both of them thinking ahead. Only when they entered the house did Reece speak up.

"Do you need to check on Miss Greer?"

"Valerie's here. Let's just sneak upstairs." Sara had never brought a man into this house for the purpose of having sex; in fact, the only time she'd slept with a man under Miss Greer's roof was two weeks ago, with Reece, while her landlady was absent. She had no idea whether her employer would object, but just now she didn't care.

All of the guest rooms were full, so Sara and Reece headed directly to her room on the third floor. Belatedly she realized she hadn't prepared for company, but she didn't figure Reece would notice. He seemed pretty single-minded at the moment.

Just the same, she didn't turn on the lights or open the shades. She closed her bedroom door, turned the lock and, still holding Reece's hand, headed directly for the bed.

Reece stopped before she reached it, tugged her to him and wrapped her in his arms. His kiss was so steamy they could have boiled lobsters without a stove. Feeling his hot mouth on hers, his hands roving anywhere and everywhere at once, she thought she might burst into flame.

He made quick work of the zipper on the back of her dress. The garment fell in a heap at her feet, and she stepped out of it and kicked it aside. In no time he had her stripped of her bra and panties. He was so efficient, in fact, that he was half undressed himself before she even realized it. She helped him with the studs on his tux shirt, her hands trembling with anticipation as heat pooled between her legs.

They fell onto the unmade bed, and for once she was glad she was a slapdash housekeeper when it came to her own space, because it would have taken too much time to pull back the covers.

She felt no need for excessive foreplay; she was so ready. She'd been ready for him for hours. She pulled him on top of her and wrapped her legs around him, and he entered her with one swift, deep thrust.

She gasped with the indescribable pleasure of joining with Reece again.

"Sara," he said on a groan. "You make me insane."

"Insane is good," she shot back, but he cut her off with another of his masterful kisses.

They rocked together in her big four-poster bed, which serenaded them with a gentle squeaking. With each of Reece's thrusts, Sara felt herself moving closer to that exquisite place that was so fine and so rare, a special place she'd never been with anyone but Reece, like their own private universe. Then the stars exploded and Sara soared through them, buoyed by wave after wave of stardust.

She was so far gone, she only vaguely registered Reece's low groan of pleasure as he joined her on their private psychic plane.

Minutes or hours later, the dimly lit room around them reappeared. Reece rolled over and cradled her against his shoulder, kissing the top of her head. "I don't know what to say."

"Then say nothing. No words are necessary."

"Can we just stay in bed the rest of the weekend?"

"We can, but we'll get hungry."

"We'll order room service."

"Unfortunately I'm the cook. I'll just have to go downstairs and fix something."

"We'll order pizza delivery."

"I like the way you think."

THEY DOZED INTO the evening. Reece woke to find Sara nuzzling his ear, and the simple act had him hard again in a matter of seconds.

"If you don't want me all over you again, you'd better stop that," he warned her.

She didn't stop, but chuckled low in her throat. "You think there's even a remote possibility I don't want you all over me?"

Apparently her appetite was no more diminished than his. He was determined, though, to make love to her, cherish her in the way she deserved, which of course he couldn't, because any man who properly cherished Sara wouldn't run out on her. But she was right, he didn't want to think about that and ruin what time they had left.

He kissed every part of her, from the inside of her elbow to the inside of her thigh and the back of her neck. With each soft pressure of his lips she sighed, until the sighs became whimpers and the whimpers grew more insistent. Still, even when he entered her he moved with slow, deliberate thrusts, building the tension until she tossed beneath him like a stormy sea.

When he could hold himself back not another second, he gave in to the most unbelievable climax he'd ever experienced. Sara, fine-tuned to him as she was, cried out at the exact instant he did. Waves of pleasure washed over them both, gradually weakening to mere ripples.

The rumble of the air-conditioning turning on made Reece realize he was cold. He grabbed the sheet and pulled it over both of them, scooping Sara against him.

"Wow. I'm speechless."

"Mmm," Reece agreed. Words would only diminish something that was so beyond what the English language could encompass.

Apparently Sara thought so, too, because she said nothing more. She just snuggled up against him, sighing contentedly. Amazingly they slept again and didn't wake up until after ten at night.

"Hey, you, wake up." Sara hit Reece with a pillow.

He grabbed the pillow and whacked her back. "Is that any way to wake up the man who wore himself out making you happy? What happened to nuzzling me awake?"

"I was afraid if I did we'd just end up wearing ourselves out again, and this woman needs sustenance."

"I'll take you out anywhere you want to go," Reece said, because he was starving himself.

"Ah, but sadly, this late nothing is open except the bars."

Truthfully, a burger from Old Salt's Bar and Grill, which was his favorite watering hole in Port C, sounded like heaven. But Sara had other ideas.

"I'll fix us something."

"Are you sure Miss Greer won't mind? I'm not even an official guest here anymore."

"I have my own stash of goodies. You can stay up here if you'd be embarrassed for Miss Greer to know we've been in my room together all these hours, making whoopie."

"Now how would she know that? We could have been up here watching TV."

"I don't own a TV."

"Reading poetry to each other, then."

"Would you really read poetry to me?" She batted her eyelashes at him. "That's so romantic."

"You're right, Miss Greer is no dummy. She would know exactly what we've been up to." And was he embarrassed about it? "Maybe I'll wait here for you."

"Okay," she said cheerfully as she slid out of bed and hunted for some clothes. "But don't you get dressed. I'll be comforted knowing you're naked in my bed, waiting for me."

"I always wanted to be a kept man."

After she left, he turned on the bedside lamp, thinking he would find something to read while he waited for Sara to bring him dinner in bed. But as the lamp illuminated the room, he got a good look at it for the first time, free from the haze of overwhelming passion that earlier had caused him to see only Sara.

Oh. Dear. God.

Sara might do a good job keeping house for the Sunsetter, but her domestic skills clearly didn't extend to her own space. Her stuff was *everywhere*. Several sets of clothes hung from the bedposts and were draped over the backs of chairs and on doorknobs. Her windowsills were lined with all kinds of plants, from cacti to trailing ivy. At least they all looked healthy. She had a tiny antique desk tucked into an alcove, but the papers on it were stacked so high they defied the laws of physics.

The box of dishes they'd bought at the antique store was shoved half under the bed; they'd taken out only the ones they needed to replace, washed them and tucked them back into Miss Greer's china cabinet.

Reece thought about his old girlfriend, Elaine, and the mild infringements her things had made at his place—the clothes she'd left in his closet, a few toiletries she'd left in the medicine cabinet, her cartons of yogurt in his fridge. He could only imagine what his apartment would look like after Sara invaded, if she ever came to visit.

He waited for a shudder of distaste to wash over him. But strangely, as he pictured her clothes strewn about his bedroom, every pot and dish in his kitchen dirty as she enthusiastically tried some new recipe, he felt nothing but mild amusement. Maybe he was loosening up. Maybe he *needed* loosening up.

Maybe Elaine had been right calling him an uptight, controlling neat freak.

But people did change. And if he could change, maybe Sara could, too. Not drastically, because then she wouldn't be Sara. But a little—just enough that they could meet in the middle.

A couple of weeks ago, he wouldn't have thought their lives could be meshed. But now? Now he was invested. Now his mind was stretching to include intriguing possibilities.

SARA HEARD the TV coming from Miss Greer's room, so she knocked lightly.

"Come in," Miss Greer called out, sounding happier than Sara could ever remember.

When she entered, Sara found her employer and Valerie in the sitting area of the large bedroom watching TV. Sara felt only a slight pang of jealousy; Miss Greer had invited Sara to relax in her private room only a handful of times in eleven years. But Valerie was a blood relative and here only temporarily. Of course Miss Greer would want to spend as much time as possible with her.

"Sorry I haven't checked in since this morning," Sara said. "Is everything okay?"

"Everything's fine, dear," Miss Greer said. "The guests are quiet."

"Good." The TV screen caught Sara's eye. "What's going on with the storm?"

"You haven't heard?" Valerie said. "It's now Hurricane Chelsea."

"And it's headed this way," Miss Greer added. "If it doesn't change course, it's supposed to make landfall early Monday morning. Maybe tomorrow you could get out the ladder and close the shutters."

She didn't sound too worried, so Sara decided she shouldn't be, either. This brick house had withstood storms for over a century, and the worst that had happened was an occasional brick or shingle coming loose.

"I'll take care of it," Sara promised. She wondered if she should mention the storm's status to Reece, then decided not to. He would only worry about it, and his flight was scheduled before the storm would hit, so it shouldn't concern him. "I'm going to fix myself some dinner and go to bed," she announced.

"Good night, dear," Miss Greer said. "Oh," she added just as Sara was about to close the door, "tell Reece good-night, too."

Sara felt her face heating as she escaped into the kitchen. She hadn't been as discreet as she'd thought. Then again, Miss Greer had a sixth sense when it came to the goings-on under her roof.

The refrigerator was stuffed full with wedding leftovers, which Valerie had generously carted back here. Sara had been too busy during the wedding to actually eat anything, but now she warmed up two big plates of the Mexican food, including Reece's special enchilada.

She was disappointed to find Reece dressed when she returned to her room with their feast. She had thought maybe they would eat naked on her bed. But Reece voted for her small table and chairs, which was suitably cozy and intimate after she cleared all the junk off it and stuck a candle in her tarnished silver candelabra.

"I'm sorry I skipped all this at the wedding," he said after inhaling the enchilada, several taquitos and some refried beans and chips. "I don't even like Mexican food, but this is wonderful."

She warmed under his praise. "Thanks. Not all Mexican food is superspicy."

"You should do more catering. I heard a lot of the wedding guests raving about how great the food was."

"I would do more, if people asked. But you have to remember, the kitchen isn't mine. I'm sure Miss Greer wouldn't mind my taking an occasional job, but I couldn't disrupt the B and B with large-scale cooking on a regular basis."

"I guess not. But it's a shame, because you could make a fortune. And you love to cook."

She'd thought about trying to make a go of catering, to really push it instead of just taking a job here or there when they fell into her lap. But that would require capital investment…a business plan…employees and taxes…advertising and marketing. All those things gave her hives.

"I like doing it whenever," Sara said, hearing herself through Reece's ears and knowing she sounded like a flake. "If I actually turned it into a business, I'm afraid it wouldn't be fun anymore."

He shrugged. "It was just a thought."

But Sara got the distinct impression she hadn't said what Reece wanted to hear. What possible difference could it make to him? He was leaving in less than twenty-four hours and he would never see her again.

She felt an almost overwhelming urge to tell him of her suspicion that she was pregnant. But she squelched it. She wouldn't manipulate him that way. At the very least, she ought to be certain before she said anything.

Following her own advice, she pushed thoughts of the future out of her mind and concentrated on the here and now. "Did you leave room for dessert? I brought up sopaipillas, but they're never very good unless they're fresh. Still, if we drown them in enough honey… What?" He was looking at her in a slightly predatory way, almost smiling but not quite.

"I was just thinking about what I *really* want for dessert."

"Oh." She smiled and reached for the hem of her T-shirt.

"Wait. I really need to go to Cooper's. My aunt and uncle will wonder what happened to me."

Sara sagged with disappointment. "You're leaving? Can't you just call and tell them you're…engaged elsewhere?"

Reece removed his glasses and absently cleaned them with his ever-present handkerchief. "It would get back to my father in two seconds."

"So? Does he think you're a monk? Why does he care what you do on the weekend?"

She could see he was thinking about it. "I at least

need to get my things. Toothbrush, razor…unless you like the caveman look."

"I like just about any look on you. Hurry back."

As HE SLID behind the wheel of his car, Reece turned his cell phone on and it immediately began to ring. He didn't answer, didn't even look at the caller ID. He knew it was someone from the family, someone who thought he ought to be on a shorter leash.

He was too content to let the Remington clan bug him. He'd never felt more relaxed, more at peace. Although he knew it wouldn't last, he wanted to hold on to the feeling a while longer, to bask in the glow of Sara's lovemaking. Monday morning they could have him back, but for now he was determined to relax and enjoy the moment.

Several cars were parked at Cooper's house and the windows were all lit up. Apparently the party lived on. That suited Reece just fine. Hopefully he could slip in and slip out without getting interrogated.

But when he entered through the front door, he didn't find a party atmosphere. A group of cousins were gathered in front of the big-screen TV watching the Weather Channel.

"Reece, there you are. About time." It was Uncle Jonathan. He had on a suit and a cell phone in each hand. "Why weren't you answering your phone?"

"I turned it off." And that was all the explanation he was going to provide. "Is something wrong?"

"Have you been living under a rock? We have a category three hurricane headed straight for us. If it stays on course, it'll make landfall at Port Clara in the early hours of Monday morning. I've rescheduled my flight for tonight and you better do the same. The airport is sure to be a madhouse."

"Hurricane? When did that happen? I thought it was just a little tropical storm way out in the gulf."

But Jonathan wasn't listening. He was talking to an airline agent, making sure he had a first-class seat.

Reece wandered toward the TV. Sure enough, that worrisome little tropical depression had organized itself into Hurricane Chelsea in record time and was gaining strength. News video clips showed people standing in line to buy gas, water and plywood for boarding up windows.

Alarm bells went off in Reece's head. If an evacuation was ordered, the roads would be clogged, the airport jammed. He had to get out of here. He had to beat the rush or he might never get home. If he missed that Monday meeting…

But then sanity prevailed. It was a hurricane. His father was just going to have to understand. He could postpone the meeting or hold it without Reece, but the world wouldn't come to an end.

At least, he didn't think so.

He thought uneasily about the phone calls he hadn't answered, and finally he couldn't resist the impulse to check. He pulled his phone out of his tux pocket. Four messages, all from his father.

"Are you going to try to get on a plane tonight?" It was Max, who was chowing down on a piece of pizza and looking perfectly relaxed. And why shouldn't he be? He didn't have to travel during a hurricane.

"I thought I would wait it out," Reece replied.

"That's what I would do. No sense making yourself crazy just to get back one day earlier." Max lowered his voice. "You don't want to travel anywhere near Uncle Jonathan. He's gone into his Tasmanian devil routine. Apparently some stupid meeting on Monday means millions of dollars one way or another."

Ugh, the meeting. Reece found a quiet corner and listened to his messages. The first was merely cautionary, pointing out that he'd better confirm his plans because travel was going to get dicey. The next call was slightly more insistent, instructing Reece to try to get an earlier flight, maybe book with a couple of different airlines so he'd be sure to make it home in time. The third call, Archie sounded angry, and the fourth, he was threatening to fire Reece if he didn't return his call.

The sharp pain in Reece's chest returned, and he rubbed his sternum absently. He shouldn't let his father get to him. The man threatened to fire Reece at least once a month. But he knew he wouldn't be able to relax with Sara unless he confronted Archie and reassured him everything was fine.

After all, he had a confirmed reservation for tomorrow evening, several hours before the hurricane was supposed to hit.

"Where the hell have you been?" were the first words out of Archie's mouth.

"With a beautiful woman," Reece answered, not in the mood to placate his father.

"Oh, yes. The maid. Well, you've had your fun and games. You better get yourself on a plane and get back here. In another couple of hours, every seat on every plane will be double-booked and you'll be stranded for days. Make no mistake, Reece, if you're not at that meeting Monday, don't bother to come back at all."

The pain in his chest grew stronger, and Reece found himself taking in great gulps of air. "I'll be there," he said, because any other answer would prolong the conversation.

"You'd better be." His father disconnected.

Chapter Thirteen

Sara got tired of listening for the sound of Reece's car. How long did it take to grab a toothbrush and razor?

She wasn't the type of woman who sat around waiting for a guy. So she got out of bed, took a quick shower, threw on her most comfortable jammies and set about cleaning her room.

As she attacked the clothing strewn all around, she tried to see her space through Reece's eyes and shuddered. Her lack of housekeeping skills had probably bothered him a lot, yet he hadn't said anything.

Reece was like her father in some ways, she realized with a start. He ran his life with an almost military precision and attention to detail. But unlike her father, he didn't criticize or expect everyone else to live up to his standards.

She knew Reece might never understand her ways, but he'd stretched out of his comfort zone to meet her halfway. The least she could do was try to do the same. Keeping her room a bit neater was a start.

She put a quick coat of furniture polish on her table

and placed a grouping of candles in the center. She was about to light them when her cell phone rang.

She knew even before she answered that it wasn't going to be good news.

"Reece?" She tried not to sound *too* anxious.

"Yes. Listen, I'm really sorry, but—"

"You're not coming back?" Her voice sounded shrill even to herself. *Deep breaths. Listen to what he has to say.*

"There's a hurricane."

"Right, Chelsea. But they don't even know if it's going to hit near here, and even if it does, it won't make landfall until Monday morning."

"You knew about the hurricane? And you didn't say anything?"

"Um…yeah. I didn't think it was that important."

Now he was the one taking deep breaths. "Well, it is important. Apparently flights are already being rescheduled, the airport is crazy—you should watch the news."

She hated watching the news. It was so depressing.

"I've got to try to catch an earlier flight," Reece continued in a harried-sounding voice. "I'm going to the airport now. I can't afford to miss my meeting on Monday. I'm already skating on thin ice."

She sighed. Maybe he was simply looking for an excuse to disentangle himself from her. Their affair had gotten pretty serious pretty fast; she'd probably scared him off with her intensity.

"Okay. Have a safe flight."

"I'm leaving the car here. You can use it until I figure out what to do with it. I'll give Max the key."

That was something, at least. "That's very generous of you. I'll take good care of it."

"If they order an evacuation, promise me you won't stay on the island."

"This house has withstood more than a hundred years' worth of hurricanes. It's not going anywhere."

"Promise me."

"All right, I promise. But it's not going to be that serious."

"Sara…there's a lot of stuff I want to say, but I don't have time now."

Ditto.

"I'll talk to you soon, okay?" He sounded agitated, and she could hear someone yelling in the background, urging Reece to hurry.

"All right. Take care."

"You, too." He disconnected, and Sara sank onto the bed, feeling like a flat tire. Was this it, then?

She'd started to believe, or at least hope, that Reece was *the one* in capital letters. She'd never felt like this about any man. She'd started to fantasize about how they could be together, even going so far as to wonder if she might learn to love New York. She'd envisioned exploring the city with Reece, going to the top of the Empire State Building, trying funky little restaurants tucked away in obscure neighborhoods—okay, maybe not that.

But clearly it wasn't going to happen. He was going home—alone. His stupid meeting was a lot more important than her, and if she was going to fall in love with some guy, he damn well better make her a priority.

She reached for the lamp, then thought about the pregnancy test she'd shoved into her bathroom cabinet. She should take it now. She wanted to know the worst.

Five minutes later, she had her answer.

She was going to have Reece's child.

Sara turned off the lights and crawled under the covers, feeling oddly peaceful. A little scared, but… happy. She'd thought it would be a disaster, but it wasn't. It was a miracle. Reece might not see it that way, though.

Oh, Lord, how was she going to tell him? On the phone? Should she fly to New York?

She hoped the answer came to her during the night.

THERE WERE TWO WAYS off the island. The short way was to take a five-minute ferry ride, the long way was to drive south for several miles, then cross a causeway.

A long line of cars waited for the ferry, ensuring at least a twenty-minute wait.

"Let's take the causeway," Reece said, too antsy to wait in line. "I don't like the ferry anyway."

"You're the boss." Max pulled a highly illegal U-turn and headed for the two-lane highway that would take them to the causeway. Traffic was pretty heavy on it, too, but at least it was moving.

"You think I'm crazy for leaving, don't you?"

"I'm thinking any guy who chooses a crowded airport over a beautiful woman waiting in bed for him is beyond crazy," Max replied.

"It's not like I'll never see her again. I'll come down to visit you guys and—"

"And she probably won't be speaking to you. Girls don't like it when you cut out on them."

"I talked to her. She wasn't mad. She's very understanding." But she had sounded disappointed. So much so, in fact, that his decision to leave had wavered slightly. Was he walking away from the best thing to ever happen to him? Would he regret choosing work over Sara, as he'd regretted his treatment of Elaine?

He'd liked Elaine, enjoyed her company, and was sad when they broke up. But that was nothing compared to the way he felt about Sara. She made him feel like…like his birthday and Christmas morning and New Year's Eve all rolled into one.

"Why do you keep rubbing your chest?" Max asked.

Reece hadn't even realized he was doing it. "I've been having chest pains."

"Are you serious?" For once, Max sounded solemn. "Have you been to a doctor? My dad had a heart attack, remember. It's nothing to fool around with if you're having symptoms."

"I'm thirty-four years old. I'm not having a heart attack. It's just…indigestion or something."

"So have it checked out. You're so anal about everything else, I can't believe you didn't see a cardiac specialist at the first twinge. Your face is kinda red."

"It's nothing." But he had to admit, at the moment it didn't feel like nothing. The pain was sharper than it had ever been before. Each breath produced a new stab, and he felt he couldn't get enough oxygen.

The roads near the airport were insane. Reece was

on standby for several flights to New York over the next few hours. Surely he would get on one of them.

But when he saw the crowd at the airport, he got a little nervous.

"I'll park and come in with you," Max said. "My bet is you aren't getting on a flight tonight."

He'd better, because tomorrow didn't look any better. The flight he had a reservation on was canceled.

By some miracle Max found a parking place. Reece grabbed his small duffel out of the minuscule trunk of Max's 'Vette, then headed for the ticket counter.

The lines were already snaking through the ticketing area. Children laughed and screamed and ran circles around the adults, most of whom barked impatiently into the cell phones glued to their ears. Even the line for first-class passengers swelled with at least thirty people, and it didn't seem to be moving.

Out of habit Reece kept an eye on his watch. He tapped his foot and willed the line to move faster. But everyone seemed to be in a bad mood, giving the poor ticket agents a hard time. It almost felt as if the atmosphere was pushing down on them all, announcing the coming storm.

He glanced up at the flight monitor. A number of flights were flashing "delayed" or "canceled."

"It's not just our weather problem," Max said. "New York is having some freakish weather. Maybe you should see if you can get a flight to some other city, rent a car and drive the rest of the way."

He didn't want to do that. He just wanted his nice, first-class seat, where he could work on his laptop and prepare for Monday's meeting. He would undoubtedly have a slew of e-mails from Bret wanting answers to this and that.

"Why's it so hot in here?" Reece grumbled. "Haven't they heard of air-conditioning?"

"It's all these people. Hey, chill out. If you don't make it home in time, Uncle Archie will just have to understand. You were best man in Cooper's wedding—it wasn't like you could just skip it. And a hurricane isn't your fault."

"Archie's vocabulary doesn't include 'understanding.'"

Finally Reece made it to the front of the line, and the agent called him.

"What's your destination today, sir?"

The pain in Reece's chest returned, the strongest it had ever been. His knees nearly buckled with the pain, he was sweating like a racehorse, and his hands and feet tingled. Hell, this wasn't indigestion.

"Sir?" the ticket agent said, looking concerned. "Your destination?"

Reece looked at Max. "The closest hospital. I think I'm having a heart attack."

THE NEXT FEW MINUTES were a blur. Max declared he could drive to the hospital faster than any ambulance, and he made good on his promise, ignoring speed limits, blasting through red lights with a honk and a prayer.

It was fortunate Reece knew where they were going and, with the help of the 'Vette's V-8 engine, they made it to the hospital in under ten minutes. Max slammed on the brakes in front of the emergency-room entrance; moments later two men in blue scrubs were dragging Reece out of the car and into a wheelchair.

He felt a little better now that they were away from the stifling air of the terminal, but his chest still felt like an elephant was sitting on it.

Before he could blink, they had him on a gurney and were stripping off his clothes.

"Hey, don't cut that!" he objected. "That's a brand-new shirt!"

In response the nurse shoved a white pill in his mouth and made him drink water, then slapped an oxygen mask over his face.

They swarmed around him like seagulls over a crust of bread, drawing blood, sticking electrodes all over his bare chest. The nurses barked out his vital signs to the doctor who'd just barged in.

"Heart rate eighty-five…"

"BP one seventy over ninety-five…"

"Oxygen saturation…"

The doctor wasn't terribly pleased, judging from his response, ordering esoteric-sounding lab tests and a chest X-ray.

Reece closed his eyes. What if he was dying? He didn't want to die yet. He had a lot of living left to do. Real living, not just existing day to day, letting his father and brother dictate his every move. His only real enjoyment, he realized, was when he lost himself in numbers.

His cousins had been right all along to ditch their jobs at Remington Industries. None of them would ever have risen much higher, not with all those older brothers. But each of them on his own—who knew what they could achieve?

If he lived through this, he was going to resign. And

he was going to tell Sara how he felt about her, and that he wanted them to be together—some way, somehow.

Oh, God, what if he never got the chance?

He opened his eyes and tried to focus them on one of the nurses. "Tell Sara I love her."

"What was that?"

Damned oxygen mask. He reached up to yank it off so he could speak properly. "Tell Sara I love her."

"Please, sir, try to relax."

Relax? When his neat, orderly life had suddenly turned into an episode of *ER?*

The nurse tried to put the oxygen mask back on, but he wouldn't allow it. This was important. "I need a phone. Get me a phone."

"Give him two milligrams of diazepam," he heard someone say, and abruptly he lost any urge to fight what was going on. He lay back on the gurney and relaxed, letting the medical professionals run their tests and talk about him as if he was no more aware than a dead fish.

Maybe this was what dying felt like. It wasn't bad.

Gradually the frenetic energy around him dissipated as one by one the nurses left, whispering.

Max entered the treatment room. He looked a bit shaken. "Jeez, Reece, you scared the hell out of me. Don't ever do that again."

"Did they give up on me? Am I about to croak or what?"

"You big goof. You weren't having a heart attack. You were having a panic attack."

"What?" That couldn't be right. Hysterical teenage

girls had panic attacks. He was Reece Remington, thirty-four-year-old financial analyst and CPA.

"The stress finally got to you, dude."

"Oh, my God. All this because I'm suffering from stress?"

"Apparently so. I told you to chill out."

"You can't tell anybody. You can't tell Archie."

"Are you kidding? Uncle Archie isn't exactly on my speed dial. But I did tell someone."

Oh, no. "Who?"

"Sara. You were yammering at the nurse that you loved her. I thought…well, I thought if there was anybody you really wanted to see…"

Reece pinched the bridge of his nose, wondering what had happened to his glasses. "Did you have to do that?"

"I thought you might die or something. Sorry."

Reece knew it wasn't Max's fault. "It's okay. I'll just call her and tell her I'm okay. Where's my phone?"

"You can't use a cell phone here."

"You call her, then. I don't want her to worry."

Someone tapped on the door. "Hello?"

Max stood. "Too late. That's my cue to take a walk."

"Bring me my duffel, okay?"

"Yeah, okay."

Sara entered the room and Max slipped out.

Reece groaned inwardly. What on earth was he going to say to her?

"What happened?" Her face was pale, her lower lip trembling. "You had a heart attack?"

Reece realized then that he was still hooked up to an I.V. drip and a couple of other machines—something measuring his heartbeat, maybe his respiration. And he was almost naked, except for underwear and a thin hospital gown.

"I didn't have a heart attack."

"Oh, thank God. What was it?"

"It was just…something else. Nothing serious."

"What was it?" she asked again.

He wasn't going to admit to Sara or anyone else that he was suffering from anxiety. Remington Industries did not promote people who couldn't handle stress. "Nothing, okay?"

She came closer and placed a hand on his forehead. It felt nice, and for a moment Reece closed his eyes and surrendered to the soft blanket of Sara's concern.

"It must have been something. Max sounded scared out of his wits when he called."

He struggled to find an explanation that would satisfy her. He didn't want to lie, but he couldn't stand having her see him like this. "I was having chest pains. But it turned out to be nothing." He removed her hand from his forehead and squeezed it. "Thank you for coming."

"Wild horses wouldn't have kept me away. I broke all kinds of laws, including a few laws of physics, to get here."

"I'm sorry you came for nothing."

"It's not nothing," she insisted. "You're hooked up to machines."

"They'll unhook me soon." Sara didn't look at all relieved. "Sara, I'm fine, really. How's the weather out there?"

"Little bit windy," she answered distractedly. "I haven't checked on the hurricane in a while."

Windy. That didn't sound good. Even if the hurricane dissipated or made landfall somewhere else, high winds here could ground a lot of planes.

He needed to get back to the airport.

"Do you have to stay at the hospital?" Sara asked.

"No, of course not. As soon as Max brings me a shirt, I'm out of here."

"And you're still planning on going to New York?"

"Yes, of course. This doesn't change anything."

"Oh."

Except something had changed. His brief brush with death—even if it hadn't been real—had forced him to realize he was in love with Sara. He'd been ready to tell her. Desperate to tell her.

But now...now was a lousy time.

"Sara, you and I aren't through."

"No?"

"No. Remember when you offered to drive my car up to New York?" he ventured. "I think it's a good idea, and I'll make it worth your while." He couldn't expect her to take off all that time from her other jobs and not be compensated.

"I thought you thought it was a terrible idea."

He shrugged.

"Well, um, I'll have to check Valerie's schedule and see how long she'll be here to take care of Miss Greer. I don't want to leave her alone, not yet."

That was when Reece realized his idea of importing Sara to New York, of keeping his job and having Sara, too, was a pipe dream. Even if she were willing to relocate, she wouldn't be happy there away from a woman who'd been like a grandmother to her, her friends, the town that had embraced her.

Besides, she had no job up there, no home. She could stay with him, but were either of them ready for that kind of commitment?

"We'll work something out."

A doctor entered the treatment room then, looking rushed and harried as E.R. doctors always seemed to. He grabbed Reece's chart from the foot of the gurney and consulted it, then smiled a bedside-manner smile that didn't exactly reassure Reece.

"Mr. Remington. You're looking better. And is this Mrs. Remington?"

"No," they both said at the same time.

Sara stepped back self-consciously. "I'm not really his wife. I said I was Mrs. Remington so I could see him."

"Sara was just leaving." He didn't want to say goodbye to her so abruptly, but neither did he want her privy to his stress issues.

"Right." She gave him a sad little smile. "Take care." She left, and it didn't feel right at all.

"Can I go now?" Reece asked impatiently.

"Not so fast. You weren't having a heart attack, but that doesn't mean you don't have some serious issues here."

Reece listened with a sinking feeling as the doctor described the state he'd been in when he arrived—gasping for breath, elevated blood pressure, racing pulse.

"We want to keep you overnight for observation.

Then we can release you, but only if you schedule some tests."

"I can't stay," Reece said. "I have to get back to New York."

"I guess you haven't heard about the hurricane."

"That's why I have to leave now. It's extremely important that I be on a plane in the next twenty-four hours."

"Well, all right," the doctor said on a sigh. "They carry defibrillators on planes now. You should be fine."

"Excuse me?"

"Mr. Remington, you're a walking time bomb. Next time, those chest pains really could be a heart attack. If you don't slow down and address your stress issues, you might not live long enough to become CEO or CFO, or whatever it is you aspire to become."

Reece closed his eyes. Good God, what was he doing to himself? Was a stupid job, or pleasing his father, worth killing himself over?

To hell with his meeting. He'd have to miss the damn thing. When the doctors cleared him, he would fly back to New York, but only for long enough to resign his job, pack up his stuff and put his condo on the market. Then he would move back to Port Clara.

He would do just what Allie had suggested. He'd start a little accounting business, maybe take up running again. He would take care of himself.

God help him, he would learn to eat exotic vegetables and whole-wheat whatever. He would take yoga classes, if that was what it took to reclaim his health.

He wanted to live to be an old man, and he wanted to do it with Sara.

SARA'S FACE WAS WET with tears as she drove back to Port Clara in Valerie's rental car. She tried to tell herself they were tears of relief that Reece wasn't dying.

But that wasn't it.

She'd been crushed with disappointment when Reece had called to tell her he was heading home early to beat the hurricane. But she'd been able to convince herself—just barely—that she shouldn't be so selfish, that Reece's job was a huge priority in his life even if she didn't understand that. Just because he was going back to New York didn't mean they were finished.

But when she'd seen him in the E.R., gorgeous even hooked up to machines, she'd seen the truth in his eyes. He hadn't wanted her there. Then he'd iced the cake. He'd told her he wanted to *pay* her to drive his car up north.

She was still Sara the B and B maid to him. Someone who needed his money, not an equal at all. Maybe they could have a good time in New York, and maybe it would never happen. But his attitude had brought everything into clear focus.

He didn't care for her the way she'd come to care for him. And if she'd learned one thing about relationships, it was that it never worked when one person was wildly in love and the other wasn't.

She was going to have to break things off with Reece. She would come up with some excuse why she couldn't drive his car to New York, and that would be that.

Oh, hell. What about the baby?

She had to tell him. But only after she'd figured a few things out, like how she was going to live and pay for things. If Reece wanted to be a part of his child's life, of course she would welcome it. But she wasn't going to be his burden, his charity case, the big mistake he would always regret.

Chapter Fourteen

By the time Reece was released from the hospital the next day, he felt he'd aged twenty years. Although the doctors had assured him there wasn't an imminent danger of dying, he'd been diagnosed with hypertension and his cholesterol was seriously out of whack.

He'd been given numerous lectures, seemingly from any doctor or nurse who felt like letting loose on some hapless patient. Loaded down with a couple of prescriptions, a number of tests he needed to schedule and a healthy eating plan he'd sworn to follow, he finally escaped from the medical profession's clutches.

Max picked him up. "How's it going?" he asked casually.

"I might live to the end of the year, at least."

"You look better."

"I feel better. Seriously." And it wasn't just because his symptoms were gone. Having made the big decision about his life, he felt as if a huge anvil had been lifted from his shoulders. His neck no longer felt stiff. He could breathe.

"So where to?"

"Airport."

"Um, you sure about that? I mean, the weather—"

"Yeah. I can't resign over the phone. I have to face Archie in person."

"All right!" Max high-fived him. "About time you saw the light. That company was going to chew you up and spit you out eventually."

"It almost did."

"So what's your hurry? There's no rush to make the meeting now. Who cares if Archie fires you?"

"It's Bret. I need to help him get ready for the promotion. But then it's over. He'll have to manage on his own."

"I wish you luck, man."

The airport was worse than before, but somehow it didn't bother Reece at all. He stood in various lines for hours, almost got on a plane at five-thirty but didn't, and returned to ticketing.

Although the hurricane had been downgraded to a tropical storm, the winds were picking up.

Unruffled, he got another reservation for Monday morning, when they believed the worst of the storm would be over. He wouldn't make the meeting, that was a given.

He called his father and gave him the bad news.

Archie reacted worse than Reece had anticipated. He yelled and cursed and threatened, but Reece just held the phone away from his ear until his father calmed down.

"I don't care how you get here," Archie said. "Take a train, car, ox-cart, but you be at that meeting or don't bother coming back at all." He hung up.

"Well, that didn't go quite as I'd hoped." Reece found a semicomfortable chair and went to sleep while the storm raged outside.

THE MEETING WAS long over by the time Reece rolled into Remington Industries' Manhattan headquarters Monday afternoon. He greeted the receptionist with a smile, wondering if they were going to stop him and call security, since he probably no longer had a job.

"Good morning, Mr. Remington," she said, smiling a little more broadly than usual. Maybe it was because she saw something in him that hadn't been there before. Something like love.

When he got to his office, he was dismayed to find it empty. Other than the battered furniture, nothing was left to indicate he had spent eight years of his life here.

He guessed his dad hadn't been kidding.

Strangely, he wasn't terribly bothered by the fact Archie had carried through with his threat. His father's actions saved him the trouble of resigning.

"You're back."

Reece whirled around to find Archibald Remington III standing right behind him, but not looking as intimidating as usual. Was that a…smile on his face?

Archie patted Reece on the shoulder. "I trust you got my nephew married off in fine form."

"Um, yeah. The wedding was great."

"I heard something about a hurricane. Is that what delayed you?"

Hadn't Reece told him that, like, six times? "Yes."

"Well, at least you're back now. Come to my office, we have things to discuss."

Dead man walking, he thought as he followed Archie down the carpeted hall. Did everyone already know?

Once inside his palatial office, Archie reached for a wooden box on his desk and held it out to Reece. "Cigar?"

Cigar? Archie had never offered Reece a cigar in his life. "I don't smoke."

"Oh, right." He snapped the box closed, then slid behind his desk and sank into his plush leather desk chair, indicating a wing chair for Reece. "I'll get down to business, then. Bret told me everything."

"Every...what?" What the hell was he talking about? How much did he know about Sara?

"Today's meeting was an unmitigated disaster. A train wreck."

"I'm sorry I couldn't be there." He genuinely was. Though he was leaving Remington Industries, he had no desire to do harm to the company or his father's department.

"Your brother came off like a flaming imbecile. Afterward, he told me you've been doing all his work for years, and he's been taking credit for it."

"Dad," Reece objected, "that's just not true."

"Yes, it is, and I should have seen it. Without you there to prop him up, Bret couldn't answer the simplest questions."

"I'm sure he's just having a bad day." Reece had never felt he was doing Bret's work for him. He'd felt more like...like the go-to guy, the one who solved sticky problems, freeing up his brother for more important things.

"He's having a bad decade," Archie declared. "There's no way he can do my job, and he freely admits it. He suggested that if I want a Remington to step into my shoes when I retire, it ought to be you. And after giving it some thought, I agree."

"Say what?"

"I'm offering you the vice presidency. The board will have to approve, of course, but they'll go along with whomever I endorse. We'll have to put in some long hours to get you ready. Are you up to it?"

"So I'm not fired?"

Archie laughed. "Fired? Where would you get that idea? Oh, your empty office. I had your things moved into Ed Jameson's old office. We'll be working closely over the next few months, and Ed's old office is closer to mine."

The corner office?

To buy time, Reece stood and walked to a side table where a pitcher of ice water and a couple of glasses had been set up. He poured some water and gulped it down.

Vice president. Reece Remington, vice president.

From a professional standpoint, it was everything he'd ever aspired to be—the title, the respect and the chance to chart a course for the company's financial future.

He let the possibility shimmer in his mind for all of fifteen seconds before he set down his glass with a thud and shook his head. "I can't do it."

"Pardon me?"

"Dad, I'm grateful you want to put your faith in me.

But I can't be a vice president. In fact, the only reason I came back here today was to turn in my resignation."

Archie gaped at him.

"The real reason I didn't make it back in time for the meeting is I was in the hospital. I'm on the short list for a heart attack if I don't get rid of the stress in my life. I'm moving to Port Clara, opening a small accounting practice, and if all goes well I'll get married and give you some more grandchildren, and I'll live long enough to see my own grandchildren."

All the color drained from Archie's face. "You're quitting? Leaving the family business just like that?"

"I've given it a lot of thought."

"You can't leave," Archie declared. "I won't let you make the biggest mistake of your life. Cooper and Max lost their minds when they quit and moved to that backwater town, but I thought you had more brains than that."

"It's the smartest thing I can do for myself," Reece said with utter certainty. He felt bad, knowing he was disappointing his father. But he would feel worse if he knuckled under to Archie's demands.

"You do understand what you're giving up? That I just offered you a *vice presidency?*"

"It wouldn't mean much if I had a heart attack and died."

Finally Reece's arguments seemed to get through to Archie. The older man pressed his lips together and gazed off into space.

"I'm sorry, Dad."

"Well…" Archie sighed. "When you put it like that…God knows your mother would never forgive me if I gave you a heart attack." He rose and walked to the window, staring out at the Manhattan skyline, and Reece gave him a few moments to absorb the news.

Finally Archie turned back to face his son, and he was smiling again, though not quite as convincingly. "So when do we meet Sara? I presume she has something to do with your decision."

"She has a lot to do with my decision—but she doesn't know it yet." He could only hope she would welcome his change of plans.

Chapter Fifteen

Sara had a bad feeling about this meeting Miss Greer had called. The two of them and Valerie sat in the kitchen, drinking tea and eating some cookies Valerie had baked. But despite the informality, Sara knew Miss Greer was going to tell her something she wasn't ready to hear.

"Miss Greer, you aren't sick, are you?" Sara blurted out.

"Oh, no, dear, I didn't mean to worry you. My hip is healing up just fine. But I'm not as young as I used to be, and keeping up with the bed-and-breakfast is getting to be too much for me. I've depended on you far too much lately, and you might not always be here if a certain young man has his way."

"Who, Reece?"

"Who, Reece, she says." Miss Greer shared a conspiratorial smile with Valerie. "So, anyway, I've decided to sell the Sunsetter."

"Oh, no!"

"Now, Sara, don't take it that way. My daughter

wants me to come live with her, and it would be crazy to say no. Imagine, after all these years with no family, I suddenly have a daughter and grandchildren who want to get to know me."

Sara struggled not to be selfish. "Of course I understand. But are you sure? You've lived here almost your whole life."

"I've run this business for sixty-odd years. I'd like to retire and enjoy whatever time I have left."

Sara could have argued that it would be cold in Michigan, that Miss Greer would miss Port Clara's balmy weather. But if Miss Greer wanted to be with her newfound family, who was Sara to argue?

"Then I'll wish you the best of luck in your new life. Can I come visit? I've never been to Michigan."

Miss Greer finally smiled. "I'm counting on it. You'll bring Reece, and the grandchildren, too."

"Grandchildren?" Sara squeaked. Did Miss Greer know something? Was Sara's pregnancy oozing from her pores?

But Miss Greer moved on. "There's something else we need to discuss."

What now? Sara didn't know if she could take any more bad news.

"I can't think of anyone I'd rather see own the Sunsetter than you. Would you be interested in buying it? I would sell it to you on very friendly terms."

"Oh! Gee, I never thought of myself owning real estate." Owning a home seemed so permanent. Yet she had called this place home for more than ten years. And now that she had another life to think about—a child who would require space and a yard to play in, maybe a dog…

"I don't know that I could swing it," she admitted. "I don't have any money for a down payment, and if I did…well, I really need a new car." She had no idea how much the B and B was worth, but she imagined it to be far out of her reach.

"Why don't we talk to my banker?"

"I'll think about it." But she was pretty sure she already knew her answer. She loved the Sunsetter. She knew every nook and cranny, every cabbage rose on the living-room curtains, every squeaky floorboard, every inch of the oak molding. But now that she'd lived here with Reece, shared meals with him in the kitchen and dining room, made love to him in his room and hers, she couldn't stay here.

She still half expected to run into him every time she rounded a corner. And though she had eradicated every scrap of his existence from his room, the smell of the soap they'd used here for years now reminded her of him.

The entire B and B had become a painful reminder of the fact he'd chosen his work over her. She'd been toying with the idea of leaving, starting something new. Only Miss Greer's dependence on her had stopped her. Now that she knew Valerie and her mother would be taking care of Miss Greer, Sara could make her own plans.

Sara tidied up the kitchen, then stepped out to the front porch to pick up the mail. There was a strange envelope addressed to her, from the Princess Cruise Line.

She almost tossed it, thinking it was junk mail. But then she remembered that she had applied for a chef's job there months ago. She tore it open and read the letter.

Holy cow. They wanted her. The job was probably low on the galley totem pole—she had nothing prestigious in her references. But on a cruise ship! It was something she'd always wanted to try.

Besides, anything beat waiting around here, thinking about Reece. The salary wasn't half-bad, and she would have health insurance. Maybe a job on a cruise ship was only a stopgap measure, but it would give her some time to think and plan.

She called the personnel director and told them she would accept the position. He instructed her to report for work the following Monday.

REECE'S PALMS FELT clammy as he boarded a plane at LaGuardia. He would fly to Dallas, where he would catch another plane to Corpus Christi. Max would meet him there and drive him to Port Clara. Then he would freshen up at Max's condo and head for the Sunsetter.

His damp hands had nothing to do with the engagement ring in his pocket. He'd never been more sure of a decision in his life. As crazy at it was, he and Sara were meant to be together. Their life together would not be without adjustments, to be sure, but it would certainly never be boring.

No, his nervousness had more to do with the fact that he hated airplanes almost as much as he hated boats.

The first flight was fine, but the short hop across Texas was a nightmare, with the plane alternately bucking and swooping until Reece's head swam. He'd never been so grateful to be on solid ground as when they finally landed in Corpus.

Until he discovered the airline had lost his luggage.

"I never check luggage for this very reason," said Max, who'd met him at the baggage claim. "Come on, let's go get something to eat. They'll send your luggage along when they find it."

"I'm too nervous to eat. Damn, I really want to change clothes before I see Sara."

"You look fine," Max said unconvincingly.

Reece decided not to worry. Surely she wouldn't let a few wrinkles in his clothes bother her. "Let's just go straight to the Sunsetter."

"You want to call and warn her you're on your way?" Max asked as they headed for his 'Vette, parked illegally at the curb.

"I've been trying to call her. She doesn't answer." Which made him even more nervous. Was she screening her calls and refusing to answer his? She often forgot to charge her phone, so he tried not to let it bother him.

"Have you even talked to her since you left?"

"No. I wanted to burn all my bridges before I talked to her."

"So if she dumps you, you won't be tempted to go back to your old job?"

"Something like that." Although it was more a case of wanting to present his resignation and relocation as a done deal. How could she refuse a man who had changed his whole life, turned down a vice presidency, all for her?

He still worried she would do just that. He hadn't felt good about their last meeting. The closer he got to his destination, the more apprehensive he felt, though he didn't notice any chest pains or shortness of breath.

When Max pulled his car up to the curb in front of the B and B, Reece had his first concrete sign that something was very wrong. A For Sale sign had been stuck in the front yard.

Max turned off the engine. "Wonder what that's about?"

Reece was damn well going to find out. He jumped out of the low-slung car and jogged to the porch and up the steps. He nearly broke his finger ringing the doorbell.

Valerie answered, but she didn't look pleased to see him there. In fact she looked almost…horrified.

"Reece! Oh, dear…"

"What? Did something happen? Did someone die?"

"Uh, no, nothing like that. Come in, please. Hi, Max."

"Where's Sara?" Reece demanded none too politely. But he was not in a polite mood.

"Maybe you better talk to my grandmother. Sara's fine, don't look so stricken. But she's not here."

Miss Greer was already making her way out, limping laboriously with the aid of a walker. She, too, appeared distraught at seeing him. "Oh, Reece. I knew Sara had gotten everything wrong."

"Where is she?"

Miss Greer all but wrung her hands. "She's gone. She took a job working in the kitchen on a cruise ship."

"Where? What cruise ship?"

Miss Greer paused, thinking, then shook her head. "I can't remember. Valerie?"

"It was the Princess line," Valerie supplied. "Out of

Los Angeles. She said she would be working the Baja cruise. But I can't remember the name of the ship."

"I'll find it."

"You're going after her?" Max asked.

"Of course I'm going after her!"

"Whoa."

"You'd better hurry," Valerie said. "The ship leaves tomorrow afternoon."

Reece turned to Max. "Take me back to the airport."

Max groaned. "Can't you just call her? Doesn't she have a cell phone?"

"She never turns the damn thing on." He would keep trying to reach her. But meanwhile, he would get to where she was as fast as humanly possible. He headed for the door.

"Reece." It was Miss Greer.

"Yes?"

"She thought you didn't return her feelings. If you don't…if you aren't serious, please don't chase after her. You'll only cause her more pain."

"I'm as serious as…" He'd started to say *as serious as a heart attack*. But he didn't joke about that kind of thing anymore. "I want to marry her. Is that serious enough?"

Miss Greer smiled. "You'll make a wonderful husband."

THE CORPUS CHRISTI AIRPORT was starting to feel like home to Reece, he'd spent so much time there lately. He managed to get the last seat on the last flight for L.A. that night, and he would have to change planes in El Paso. But with any luck he would make it to the cruise ship in time.

Unfortunately, luck wasn't on his side. His flight was delayed due to weather—again!—and by the time he arrived in El Paso he'd missed the connection. The next plane for L.A. wouldn't leave until morning and, though technically he would still make it in time, he didn't want to trust his fate to weather and the whims of airline schedules.

He would rent a car, that was it. But the first rental car place he tried was out of cars.

"How can you be out of cars?"

The uncaring woman behind the counter shrugged. "It happens. Big convention of manufactured housing salesmen cleaned us out. I doubt you'll find a rental car anywhere at the airport."

"Where ya headin'?" asked a scruffy-looking man who'd been eavesdropping.

"L.A."

"I'm goin' that direction. I'll take you with me if you'll buy the gas."

"Deal."

Reece's new best friend was named Red, and Red's car looked like it was held together with rubber bands and duct tape. Red wasn't exactly a scintillating conversationalist, and his taste in music—some kind of heavy metal—threatened to give Reece a migraine. But Red drove fast, and that was all that mattered.

Halfway across the desert, he pulled off the highway onto a side road.

Reece roused himself from a half-sleep. "Why are we stopping?"

"This is as far as I'm going."

"What?"

"I'm sure you can get a ride from here."

Oh, God. He'd never hitchhiked in his life. He looked at his watch. "Is there an airport near here?"

"If there was, I'd have flown instead of driving."

Fine. He'd hitchhike. "Thanks for getting me this far," he said grudgingly as he got out.

Hitchhiking wasn't as easy as it looked. For one thing, at four in the morning the traffic on this road wasn't exactly brisk. When cars did come along, they sped past without sparing him a glance, and could he blame them? He would never pick up a hitchhiker.

At dawn the growl of half-a-dozen motorcycle engines approached from behind, and Reece didn't bother sticking his thumb out. But one of the bikers pulled up beside him anyway.

"Need a ride, stranger?"

The biker was a woman. A big woman. A couple of her friends had stopped, too.

"Um…" He looked at his watch. Hell, why not? "Sure. Thanks."

The woman gave him her extra helmet. "Lucky you don't have luggage."

"Yes, I…" Oh, hell. He'd left his small duffel in the scruffy man's trunk. He'd been so focused on being stranded he'd forgotten all about the bag.

At least he still had his wallet. He climbed on behind the woman, wondering if he'd lost his mind as well as his heart.

"Hold on tight, handsome." And off they went. Reece grabbed on to the woman's thick middle at the last moment. The only saving grace was, with the loud engines and the wind, conversation was impossible.

Biker woman and her friends took him all the way to Los Angeles, but not before riding through a rainstorm that soaked Reece through the skin, turning the road grime sticking to him into mud. The sun was high in the sky by the time he reached Long Beach and the L.A. Harbor, looking and feeling like a degenerate.

Twenty minutes of searching and asking, and he finally found the *Sapphire Princess,* bound for Baja. Thank God, it hadn't left yet. A glass-enclosed building led to the gangway, and that was where he hit another roadblock. He couldn't board without a ticket.

"But I'll be getting right back off again. I just need to find someone."

"Yeah, right," said the unsmiling ticket-taker, who could have played a bouncer in a rough bar.

"Then where can I buy a ticket?"

The bouncer looked Reece up and down, obviously doubting he belonged on a luxury cruise ship. "Easiest way would be to find a computer terminal, order online and print out your boarding pass. But we close the gangway for good in twenty minutes."

Reece tipped his head back and looked up at the sky. Why, oh, why did Sara not answer her cell phone?

But then he spied an Internet café—right there at the harbor.

IT DIDN'T TAKE Sara long to unpack—it never did. Her quarters on the *Sapphire Princess* were distinctly unglamorous, a closet-size room with a tiny bunk, a tiny dresser and a tiny sink with a tiny mirror. Honestly, the cabin had been designed for Thumbelina, and the bathroom was down the hall.

This was quite a comedown from her quarters at the Sunsetter B and B, and it didn't even have a porthole.

But she wouldn't spend much time here. She would be busy. She was expected to work long hours, which was fine with her. The harder she worked, the less time she had to think about Reece.

One problem, though. All through her first shift she'd suffered from morning sickness. Even now she was queasy, and though she longed for a nap after her shift cutting up fruit for a buffet, she needed fresh air worse than sleep.

She now had an inkling of why Reece didn't like boats.

She was about to head for the deck when someone knocked at her door. Curious, she opened it and found Reece Remington standing there. Only it wasn't the Reece Remington she was accustomed to. This one wore wrinkled, disheveled, filthy clothes, uncombed hair and a day's growth of beard.

Her jaw dropped and her heart pounded crazily. "Reece? What are you doing here?"

"I'm trying not to be sick."

Join the club.

But then he smiled. "I can't believe I found you." He steadied himself against the doorway. "Is the boat moving?"

It was. And her stomach was pitching right along with it. "Follow me. Up on deck." Otherwise, things were going to get very unpleasant.

Once she could breathe the fresh air and see the sky, she felt better. She stood at the railing, oblivious to the hubbub around her as the *Sapphire Princess* pulled away from the dock.

"Are you seasick?" asked Reece, standing right beside her, his hands gripping the railing just as hers were.

"Unfortunately. Never expected this."

He reached into his pocket and handed her a small bottle. "Take some Dramamine. It helps a little."

"Maybe later." After she read the label and found out whether pregnant ladies could take it.

Finally the reality of the situation sank in. Reece was here. He'd followed her here. "Did you buy a ticket?" she asked.

"I had to. But I'd have done anything to get to you. I couldn't stand to be apart from you another minute."

Was he really saying this? Was she dreaming?

He grasped her shoulders and swiveled her around to face him. "Sara, I'm so sorry I gave you the wrong impression."

Her eyes filled with tears, remembering their last conversation at the hospital. "You acted like you were trying to get rid of me."

"I was, but just for the moment. I didn't want you to know what was really wrong with me."

"What *is* wrong?" Oh, God, was he dying? Was her baby going to grow up without a father?

"Nothing, now." He smiled. "Sara, I love you so much. It took me two planes, three cars and a motor-cycle to get here so I could tell you that. I quit my job. They offered me the vice presidency, can you imagine?

And I quit. Because I don't want to live like that any-more. I want to live in Port Clara with you."

"But I don't live there anymore!" she wailed, because she was so overwhelmed she didn't know which way was up. He loved her. He'd clearly been through some kind of hell to get here, judging from the looks of things. He'd gotten on a cruise ship for her, and he hated boats.

"Then I'll go wherever you go," he declared. "If you want to live on a cruise ship, then I will, too. I'll learn to eat strange food and I'll try new things. I promise I will. And I'll love you forever if you'll marry me."

He reached into his sad-looking, shrunken jacket and pulled something out. Then he took her left hand and slid a ring onto her third finger. "Sara Kaufman, will you marry me?"

That just made her cry harder, and he drew her to him and wrapped his arms around her. "Sara, please."

Miss Greer must have told him. At the last minute, Sara had confessed to both Valerie and her grandmother about the baby. Sara couldn't explain Reece's odd behavior any other way.

"I'm sorry I'm crying so much, ruining a perfectly good moment," she said, gathering herself together. "It's my hormones. I'd always heard that pregnant ladies are weepy, but—"

Reece grasped her shoulders and pushed her away, just far enough that he could look into her face. *"Pregnant ladies?"*

"You…you didn't know?"

"How would I know something like that? I'm not psychic. So are you?"

She nodded.

"Oh, baby!" He kissed her then, like he meant it, and for the first time Sara really understood what Allie meant when she said two people could become one.

She hugged Reece hard. "You're okay with that?"

"Okay? I think it's great."

"But it's so…unplanned."

He stroked her tear-damp cheek with his knuckles. "I'm learning to roll with the punches." His gaze flickered to the rapidly receding shoreline. "Holy cow, we're stuck on this ship, aren't we."

"Yup. For a whole week." She grinned impishly at him.

"Could be worse."

"Could be a whole lot worse."

"Does this ship have some place I can buy some clothes? And a toothbrush?"

"Let me get this straight. You rode a motorcycle across the country…with no toothbrush?"

"I left my bag in the trunk of a 1964 Nova, somewhere in the desert."

With a grin Sara hooked her arm through his. "You can buy anything you need on this boat, including enough seasick medicine for an army. I'll show you around."

They started walking, but Reece stopped abruptly. "Sara, did you say yes? To the proposal, I mean."

She held out her hand to admire her engagement ring. The enormous marquis diamond winked in the sun. "Of course I'll marry you. I'll learn how to cook food you love, and I'll even open a retirement account."

She turned to face him, serious now. "I love you, Reece."

She knew their relationship would always provide challenges. But Sara loved a challenge.

Epilogue

Sara stood in the Sunsetter's front yard, admiring the new sign. The bed-and-breakfast's placard had been re-painted to include two new shingles underneath: Reece Remington, CPA, and Sea Breeze Catering.

As soon as she and Reece had finished their cruise, they had returned to Port Clara and had a long meeting with a banker. It turned out she *could* afford to buy the B and B with a little help from Reece. He'd set up his office in a side parlor.

She wasn't too sure about the catering thing, but Reece had urged her to at least give it a try. If it proved too much, she could scale back or hire a helper. She had already hired a part-time housekeeper.

Max was busy coming up with marketing plans for all three businesses.

It had been difficult to say goodbye to Miss Greer. But the woman Sara had come to think of as a grand-mother had seemed so happy, off to start a new life with her new family. Sara thought of her often, sur-rounded by grandchildren, getting stronger on her new hip every day. They'd already made plans for a visit in the fall.

"I never thought I'd own a bed-and-breakfast." Reece stood behind Sara, his arms around her, his chin resting on her shoulder.

"I didn't, either. But when you think about it, it suits me perfectly. I love being a hostess, meeting new people, cooking. It's like a party every day. I can still travel—I just have to plan in advance."

"You're sure you want to have the wedding here?"

"Absolutely." The wedding was in exactly one week. Allie, recently returned from her honeymoon, was horrified that they didn't have more time to plan. But Sara didn't care. So long as her friends and family were here to witness her and Reece exchange vows, and she had plenty of good food and drink on hand, everything would be fine.

In fact, everything was already fine. She'd gone to a doctor who had confirmed the pregnancy and pronounced her healthy as a horse; once she got off that blasted ship, she hadn't been bothered by morning sickness. When they'd learned she was pregnant, the cruise line had been happy to let her resign.

She had everything she never even knew she wanted—a home and a mortgage, a child on the way, and a man to love for the rest of her life.

* * * * *

Be sure to look for Max Remington's story,
THE GOOD FATHER,
available in April 2009
from Harlequin American Romance!

Silhouette Desire kicks off 2009 with
MAN OF THE MONTH,
a yearlong program featuring incredible heroes
by stellar authors.

When Navy SEAL Hunter Cabot returns home for some much-needed R & R, he discovers he's a married man. There's just one problem: he's never met his "bride."

Enjoy this sneak peek at Maureen Child's
AN OFFICER AND A MILLIONAIRE.
Available January 2009
from Silhouette Desire.

One

Hunter Cabot, Navy SEAL, had a healing bullet wound in his side, thirty days' leave and, apparently, a wife he'd never met.

On the drive into his hometown of Springville, California, he stopped for gas at Charlie Evans's service station. That's where the trouble started.

"Hunter! Man, it's good to see you! Margie didn't tell us you were coming home."

"Margie?" Hunter leaned back against the front fender of his black pickup truck and winced as his side gave a small twinge of pain. Silently then, he watched as the man he'd known since high school filled his tank.

Charlie grinned, shook his head and pumped gas. "Guess your wife was lookin' for a little 'alone' time with you, huh?"

"My—" Hunter couldn't even say the word. *Wife?* He didn't have a wife. "Look, Charlie…"

"Don't blame her, of course," his friend said with a wink as he finished up and put the gas cap back on. "You being gone all the time with the SEALs must be hard on the ol' love life."

He'd never had any complaints, Hunter thought, frowning at the man still talking a mile a minute. "What're you—"

"Bet Margie's anxious to see you. She told us all about that R and R trip you two took to Bali." Charlie's dark brown eyebrows lifted and wiggled.

"Charlie…"

"Hey, it's okay, you don't have to say a thing, man."

What the hell could he say? Hunter shook his head, paid for his gas and, as he left, told himself Charlie was just losing it. Maybe the guy had been smelling gas fumes too long.

But as it turned out, it wasn't just Charlie. Stopped at a red light on Main Street, Hunter glanced out his window to smile at Mrs. Harker, his second-grade teacher who was now at least a hundred years old. In the middle of the crosswalk, the old lady stopped and shouted, "Hunter Cabot, you've got yourself a wonderful wife. I hope you appreciate her."

Scowling now, he only nodded at the old woman—the only teacher who'd ever scared the crap out of him. What the hell was going on here? Was everyone but him nuts?

His temper beginning to boil, he put up with a few more comments about his "wife" on the drive through town before finally pulling into the wide, circular drive leading to the Cabot mansion. Hunter didn't have a clue what was going on, but he planned to get to the bottom of it. Fast.

He grabbed his duffel bag, stalked into the house and paid no attention to the housekeeper, who ran at him, fluttering both hands. "Mr. Hunter!"

"Sorry, Sophie," he called out over his shoulder as he took the stairs two at a time. "Need a shower, then we'll talk."

He marched down the long, carpeted hallway to the rooms that were always kept ready for him. In his suite, Hunter tossed the duffel down and stopped dead. The shower in his bathroom was running. His *wife?*

Anger and curiosity boiled in his gut, creating a churning mass that had him moving forward without even thinking about it. He opened the bathroom door to a wall of steam and the sound of a woman singing— off-key. Margie, no doubt.

Well, if she was his wife… Hunter walked across the room, yanked the shower door open and stared in at a curvy, naked, temptingly wet woman.

She whirled to face him, slapping her arms across her naked body while she gave a short, terrified scream.

Hunter smiled. "Hi, honey. I'm home."

* * * * *

Be sure to look for
AN OFFICER AND A MILLIONAIRE
by USA TODAY *bestselling author Maureen Child.*
Available January 2009 from Silhouette Desire.

CELEBRATE
60 YEARS
OF PURE READING PLEASURE
WITH **HARLEQUIN®**!

We'll be spotlighting a different series
every month throughout 2009
to celebrate our 60th anniversary.
Look for Silhouette Desire® in January!

Collect all 12 books in the Silhouette Desire®
Man of the Month continuity, starting in
January 2009 with *An Officer and a Millionaire*
by *USA TODAY* bestselling author
Maureen Child.

*Look for one new Man of the Month title
every month in 2009!*

www.eHarlequin.com   SDMOMBPA

REQUEST YOUR FREE BOOKS!

2 FREE NOVELS PLUS 2
FREE GIFTS!

Love, Home & Happiness!

YES! Please send me 2 FREE Harlequin® American Romance® novels and my 2 FREE gifts (gifts are worth about $10). After receiving them, if I don't wish to receive any more books, I can return the shipping statement marked "cancel." If I don't cancel, I will receive 4 brand-new novels every month and be billed just $4.24 per book in the U.S. or $4.99 per book in Canada. That's a savings of close to 15% off the cover price! It's quite a bargain! Shipping and handling is just 25¢ per book, along with any applicable taxes.* I understand that accepting the 2 free books and gifts places me under no obligation to buy anything. I can always return a shipment and cancel at any time. Even if I never buy another book from Harlequin, the two free books and gifts are mine to keep forever.

154 HDN EEZK   354 HDN EEZV

Name _____ (PLEASE PRINT) _____

Address _____ Apt. # _____

City _____ State/Prov. _____ Zip/Postal Code _____

Signature (if under 18, a parent or guardian must sign)

Mail to the **Harlequin Reader Service:**
IN U.S.A.: P.O. Box 1867, Buffalo, NY 14240-1867
IN CANADA: P.O. Box 609, Fort Erie, Ontario L2A 5X3

Not valid to current subscribers of Harlequin® American Romance® books.

Want to try two free books from another line?
Call 1-800-873-8635 or visit www.morefreebooks.com.

* Terms and prices subject to change without notice. N.Y. residents add applicable sales tax. Canadian residents will be charged applicable provincial taxes and GST. Offer not valid in Quebec. This offer is limited to one order per household. All orders subject to approval. Credit or debit balances in a customer's account(s) may be offset by any other outstanding balance owed by or to the customer. Please allow 4 to 6 weeks for delivery. Offer available while quantities last.

Your Privacy: Harlequin is committed to protecting your privacy. Our Privacy Policy is available online at www.eHarlequin.com or upon request from the Reader Service. From time to time we make our lists of customers available to reputable third parties who may have a product or service of interest to you. If you would prefer we not share your name and address, please check here. ☐

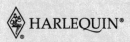

HARLEQUIN®

American ★ Romance®

TINA LEONARD
The Texas
Ranger's Twins

Men Made in America

The promise of a million dollars has lured
Texas Ranger Dane Morgan back to his family
ranch. But he can't be forced into marriage to
single mother of twin girls, Suzy Wintertone,
who is tempting as she is sweet—can he?

**Available January 2009
wherever books are sold.**

LOVE, HOME & HAPPINESS

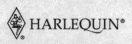

HARLEQUIN®

American ★ Romance®

COMING NEXT MONTH

#1241 THE TEXAS RANGER'S TWINS by Tina Leonard
Men Made in America
Texas Ranger Dane Morgan has been lured home to Union Junction by the
prospect of inheriting a million dollars. All he needs to do is live on the
Morgan ranch for a year…and marry Suzy Winterstone. While the sassy single
mother of toddler twin daughters is as tempting as she is sweet, no Ranger
worth his salt can be forced into marriage by a meddling matchmaker! *Can he?*

#1242 MILLION-DOLLAR NANNY by Jacqueline Diamond
Harmony Circle
When her con man ex-fiancé takes off with all her money, Sherry LaSalle finds
herself in need of something she's never had before—a job! The socialite may
have found her calling, though, as a nanny for Rafe Montoya's adorable twin niece
and nephew. The sexy mechanic couldn't be more different than the ex-heiress, but
there's something about Sherry that's winning over the kids…and melting Rafe's
heart.

#1243 BABY ON BOARD by Lisa Ruff
Baby To Be
Kate Stevens is interviewing daddy candidates. Applicants must be kind, must
be stable and must be looking for the same white-picket-fence life Kate has
always dreamed of. Unfortunately for her, fun-loving, risk-taking world traveler
Patrick Berzani—the baby's biological father—wants to be considered for the
position.…

#1244 MOMMY IN TRAINING by Shelley Galloway
Motherhood
The arrival of a megastore in Crescent View, Texas, is horrible news for
Minnie Clark. Her small boutique is barely making a profit, plus she has
the added responsibility of providing for her young niece. So when Minnie
discovers that her high-school crush, Matt Madigan, works for the megastore,
the new mommy is ready for battle!

HARCNMBPA1208